Parallel Reality
Stalked by a Shadow of the Past

William M. Selvey

with

Deb W. Childs

Parallel Reality: Stalked by a Shadow of the Past

Copyright ©2018 William M. Selvey and Deb W. Childs

Library of Congress Control Number: 2018951369

ISBN:0996579133
ISBN-13:978-0-9965791-3-1
Published by
Childs Communications
Printed in the United States of America

Cover Design by Midori Batten

DEDICATION

In Loving Memory of My Wonderful One and Only,
BERTIE SUE SELVEY

ACKNOWLEDGMENTS

My deepest gratitude goes to Deb Childs for her extensive editorial insights, which helped create a better version of my original idea and her knowledgeable publishing assistance that brought the story forth in book form.

I would also like to extend my sincere appreciation to the very talented Midori Batten for her artwork and design of the book's cover.

Many thanks also to Deborah Hocutt for her early review of the manuscript, her encouragement, and her wise advice.

‖

PROLOGUE

"What the hell were we thinking?" Tom asks his best friend in the world.

"Got me," Will said, his voice a barely-audible whisper. "We should've stayed in that little room and waited for our flight."

Both men ran as fast as they could down the narrow, rocky path trying hard not to trip and tumble off the side of the steep mountain. They had no way to know if they were being chased by the delusional fool lost in time.

"Lord, I hope we're almost there," said Tom. He could barely breathe through the panic tightening his chest. "Please God, help us get back to Richmond."

"And if we do get back, I'm done with adventure. I'll be more than happy with the safety and security of my boring, everyday life. The last damn thing I ever want to do again is run from a lunatic…" Will's voice trailed off as Tom jolted to a sudden stop in front of him.

"Did you hear that?"

The men could see before them the beginning of the path that promised to lead them back to the safety of the airport. But that vision has quickly become a blur, as they watch the Japanese man step out of the brush and directly onto the path in front of them. He boasts a smug, angry grin. Instead of a clear path back to safety, they stare directly into the barrel of a gun.

Still wearing his WWII flight uniform, did he intend to arrest them or kill them this time? Suddenly, it was uncertain if the friends would ever get back to their homes in Richmond or remain stuck in a time warp from which there was no return.

||

CHAPTER ONE
Two Friends with a Plan

It was late afternoon, March 1992. Will Sellers was finally free of the usual Monday chaos in his position as Hospital Administrator of a children's hospital in Richmond, Virginia. Looking over his dreaded list of calls to return, he noticed the phone number of his good friend, Tom Lyman. Tom worked as a CPA at the hospital and was Will's neighbor in an affluent, historic district of the city.

Instinctively, Will knew what the call was about. A few nights ago over dinner with their wives, Tom had unleashed the crazy notion to go backpacking in the Appalachian Mountains. Will wasn't too sure about the idea. He had never even camped in his own backyard, much less the Virginia wilderness. So, hiking the highest peaks in Virginia's Blue Ridge Mountains, the oldest mountain range in North America, for even a few of its 1600 miles, seemed like an over-the-top idea.

Will picked up the phone to return Tom's call, and as if he didn't already know the answer to the question, he asked, "Hey, what's up, buddy?"

"Hey, listen—I just finished reading an article called, *'All about Backpacking and How to Get Started.'* Will, I really believe this is something we would enjoy. You know it's 1992, and last I checked, we weren't getting any younger. We need to get on with living life to the fullest. Tell you what, I'll drop the article off for you to read, and if you're interested we'll go for it; deal? Just think—wide-open spaces, clean air, and a huge sky full of stars. Read the article, and let me know what you think," said Tom, barely taking a breath between sentences.

It was just like Tom to be excited about backpacking. He was the rough and tumble outdoorsman of the two friends, and he didn't mind laying down a curse word here and there. Will, on the other hand, sported a somewhat more genteel nature and rarely let a curse word pass his lips, especially around ladies. But he wasn't opposed to trying new things, and he was always up for Tom's adventurous ideas. The personality differences between the two were probably what gave their friendship its richness.

Early the next morning, Will's wife, Ann, found the article that Tom left on the back porch. As the saying goes, 'backdoor friends are best,' and that's what Tom and his wife, Michele, were for Ann and Will. It was such a blessing when they moved into the neighborhood, their homes just yards apart in the back. The men became friends when Tom began working at Will's hospital, and it was Will who helped the Lyman's find their new home next to them.

Ann sat down in the kitchen and read the backpacking article over her morning coffee. Her first impression was to encourage Will to join Tom in the adventure sport of backpacking. She thought the new hobby would be a healthy one that would give her husband some time away from the many problems related to his work at the hospital.

Later that day, Ann heard the front door open and knew it was Will, home from work.

"Ann, where are you?"

"Kitchen."

After a warm, hello hug for his wife, Will said, "Boy am I glad to be home. What a day."

"Rough day, hon?"

"It was a one-thing-after-another kind of day. But it could've been worse. How about you? You have a nice day?"

"Nothing special. Sit down and relax while I fix you a cup of tea or a glass of wine—what'll it be?"

"Tea, no sugar. Thanks."

"I'll start the water," Ann said. "The mail's there on the table. Oh yeah, there's also an article Tom left you."

"Good, I was expecting it. Leave it to Tom—always on the ball—especially when he has an idea on his mind. Maybe you'd like to read the article after me."

"I've already read it," Ann surprised Will. "It's a good article—short and to the point with a well-organized plan for beginners. I think backpacking sounds like it'd be a good thing for you guys to do."

"Not something for you girls to consider, huh?"

"I can't see me doing it, but definitely not unless Michele went, too."

Michele and Ann had become just as close friends as their husbands. It made for great ease having friends as neighbors, and they often did things together as couples.

Will chuckled at Ann's analysis of backpacking.

After breakfast on the following day, Will was ready to get right on the backpacking decision. Tom picked up on Will's first ring, as if he'd been sitting by the phone, tapping his toes.

"What took you so long? You ready to go backpacking?"

"Good morning to you, too, my friend. Come on over, and let's weigh the pros and cons of this idea."

"Pros and cons? Aw, the hell with pros and cons, my mind's already made up. I'm ready for some adventure. Let's go backpacking! How about it?"

"Whew. Okay, I'll bite, and that reminds me—at the first sign of snakes, I'm done," said Will.

"Snakes are going to be the least of your worries, man," Tom shot back, without thinking. Then realizing he might've spooked Will, he added, "Aw, don't worry, I'll take care of you."

5

The two friends had done some pretty wild things in their day to savor the fountain of youth. Will was no doubt remembering their last attempt, which found them high-mountain skiing. He spent the next six weeks nursing a broken ankle, but he would be the first to admit, they had the time of their lives before his fall.

"Sounds like we'll need a lot of equipment for backpacking; where do you get all that stuff?"

"I've already got that covered. I know the manager of the local Blue Ridge Mountain Sports store. Andy's, without a doubt, the best backpacking expert I know. I'll give him a call."

Will was completely overwhelmed as he entered the massive sports store. He'd never seen such a display of outdoor equipment. All three floors were filled from floor-to-ceiling with fishing rods and reels, hiking and skiing clothing, shoes, scuba-diving gear, tents, and the list went on and on.

Dazed, Will noticed Tom and a tall stocky man standing at the second-floor railing. Tom was waving wildly for Will to come up the stone-lined staircase. The men waited for Will in front of rows and rows of backpacks and tents that lined the aisles and walls behind them. Will was trying hard not to revisit his hasty decision in agreeing to Tom's idea, thinking now that this store, alone, would have been an adequate adventure in backpacking for him.

"Hey there, Will, nice to meet you. I'm Andy," the man said, extending his hand.

Compared to Will's five-foot-ten, moderately-fit frame, Andy was a beast at six-foot-four, wide-chested with biceps that could easily model workout equipment. It was instantly obvious that Andy took his physical fitness seriously.

Will returned his firm handshake, "Nice to meet you, too. Tom tells me you know all there is to know about backpacking, and I'm having no doubt about that at all," Will said, glancing around at all the equipment.

"I don't know if I'd consider myself an expert, but I've logged many a mile in these Salomon's," Andy said, looking down proudly at his well-worn hiking boots.

"Don't let him kid you, Will, this man's a beast when it comes to backpacking."

With eyebrows raised, *my thoughts, exactly,* Will mused to himself. After almost an hour and a half of guiding the two men through row-after-row of camping gear, Will felt confident that Andy knew this sport inside and out.

"Look, if you guys are really serious about backpacking 'The Trail,' I'll be happy to coach you through a few things. I can quickly make you a list of everything you'll need for it," Andy offered.

Tom shot a hopeful look at Will, who immediately obliged with a nod of agreement. He knew there was no turning back on Tom, now that they were in the candy store of backpacking.

"You have yourself a deal, my friend," Tom said, excitedly turning to shake Andy's hand.

Andy spent the next twenty minutes, or so, pulling specific items from the shelves while creating what looked like a mountain of gear to lug around for their new adventure to Will. If Tom was the optimist, Will was the realist of the two friends, and he began wondering how in the world they would be able to tote all this backpacking paraphernalia while hiking through the Virginia Mountains. But nobody else seemed concerned, so he let it go.

"I think I've got you guys all set on your gear here," Andy said, as he finished up. "Now let me show you how to pack it, so it'll be manageable."

Exceptional idea, thought Will, who was amazed as they watched Andy pack so much stuff into such relatively small backpacks.

"Now, a word of caution for you guys. Backpacking can be tricky. Those mountains can be downright dangerous if you don't know what you're doing. Many packers have learned things the hard way.

"I have a few tips to help you avoid some major pitfalls: Drinking water—don't assume just because water in a small creek bubbles over rocks, it's safe to drink; it isn't. Drink bottled water, or use the treatment kit I have here. Personally, I would use the kit," Andy said, stuffing it into a side pocket of the pack.

"Okay, about fire—wind can change a campfire in a heartbeat. Embers that appear to be out can be quickly whipped into hot coals. And never take an open flame, like a candle for example, into your tent.

"Now this one may sound crazy, but before making camp at night, be sure to check out the area around you. I've heard of campers who made that mistake and found out the hard way in the morning that they'd been sleeping on the edge of a steep cliff. Not something you want to find out while you're wandering around in the dark to relieve yourself—know what I mean?" Andy was smiling, but his serious tone left the impression that this advice was not something to just blow off.

His next tip broached a subject of great interest to both Will and Tom.

"And then, there are the bears. There's a big difference between black bears and brown bears. Black bears in Virginia don't normally attack people, unless cubs are involved, and there aren't any brown bears here. But in other states, like say Alaska, both brown and black bears commonly attack people, so all bears there are very dangerous. I'd suggest you always be on the alert for bears, no matter where you are. Every night, you should bag all your food and hoist it as high as you can in a tree. Bears are notorious for scavenging campsites for food."

"Hell, if I see or hear a bear, I'm running for the car," Tom admitted.

"Worst thing you can do, man," Andy said. "You couldn't outrun most bears if you tried. One thing you *can do* is freeze.

No movement or sound. Or, you can make a lot of noise and movement to let the bear think that you can be aggressive. If you're lucky, he might just leave. Try climbing a tree if any are available. You don't want the bear sizing you up for his next meal."

Then, as if to lighten up the scary bear tips, Andy threw in a joke.

"You know how to tell if a bear is a black or a brown?" he asked. "You climb a tree. If it's a black, he'll climb up the tree to get you. If he's a brown, he'll hug the tree trunk and shake you out of it."

All three men laughed, but Will wondered if there might be more truth than fiction in that story.

"The point of the joke is, brown bears don't climb trees; blacks do, but it also shows *all* bears can be dangerous, whether they climb trees or not," Andy said, as he finished inserting all the items into their new backpacks.

"We really appreciate everything, Andy," Tom said.

"Yes, thanks a lot," Will agreed. "You definitely know your stuff."

"Just be safe out there, guys. You never know what you'll run up on when backpacking. That's why it's called an adventure sport. You just never know."

Tom and Will stopped off at Charlie's Bar and Grill to plan their first trip. They had been coming to this place for drinks, on and off, for years. They sat near the back where two large pool tables stood. It was loud with a crowd, as usual.

"Ann okay with you being gone for a couple weeks?" Tom asked.

"Heck, she read the article before I did. She likes the idea of us backpacking. It'll give her time to herself, too. She'll keep herself busy reading mystery novels and solving murders on that *Dateline* show she loves so much.

"That's interesting. I didn't know that about Ann."

"Yeah, I think Nancy Drew must have been her childhood heroine," Will laughed. "What about Michele?"

"She told me to do whatever makes me happy. By the way, Will, how's your grandfather? The last time I asked, you said he wasn't doing very well. I hope he's better."

"I don't know, Tom. He's getting up in years and has some medical issues. But, all and all, I guess he's about as well as can be expected. He seems to be hanging in there."

The men ordered drinks and went over the schedule for the trip. With the equipment part of the program taken care of, they would be heading off to 'The Trail' in less than a week. Will was really looking forward to some downtime to clear his head of the normal, everyday stress that comes with being a hospital administrator. Tom just longed for his next adventure in the big outdoors.

||

CHAPTER TWO
Honorable Memories

After a long, tiring day at the office, Will was already winding down in his mind to a tall glass of red wine with Ann outside on their deck. With the backpacking trip fast approaching, just a few short days away, he wanted to spend some quality time with his wife before leaving.

"Ann," Will called out as he walked through the front door, placing his briefcase on the side table in the foyer.

No answer. Heading upstairs, Will found Ann in their bedroom, packing suitcases.

"Hey, what's up? You planning to skip town on me?" Will teased his wife of five years.

Ann turned around, and instantly Will saw that something was wrong. Her face was streaked with makeup, as tears ran down her cheeks; her eyes red and puffy.

Will rushed to her and wrapped his arms around her in a hug of compassion. "What's wrong?" he asked.

"I got a call from your grandmother about an hour ago."

Will knew what was coming next. His grandfather had been in poor health for some time, and this was the moment he'd been dreading. The two men had always been very close, and even though Will knew his grandfather was sick, he hadn't been able to bring himself to face the idea that one day this call would come, and he'd have to accept it.

"Will, your grandfather passed away this morning. I'm so sorry."

Will knew of death only through the eyes and heartbreak of others. He had yet to experience such sadness and grief over the loss of a loved one, especially one as close as his grandfather. He could feel his knees become putty. Will wasn't sure just what to do. His first instinct was just to take a deep breath, stand tall, and be the rock that he thought everyone would expect of him. He wasn't at all sure that was humanly possible, and his doubt showed all over his face.

"I didn't get to say goodbye," he mumbled in a weak and shaky voice. His legs couldn't hold him up another minute, and he dropped to the corner of the bed. Will sat with his head in his hands, as he tried his best to control the range of emotions coursing through his body.

Thoughts came flooding into his mind. *Why didn't I know it was going to be this soon? Why didn't I go visit him just one more time? I didn't get to tell him how much he meant to me.*

Ann reached out and placed her hand lovingly on her husband's shoulder. "I told your grandmother that we'd be there in the morning. I've got most everything packed."

"I have to call her," Will moaned.

"Honey, the doctors have given her something to help her sleep. She needs to rest. I've booked tickets for the red-eye, so we can be there first thing in the morning."

Will looked at Ann through tears of grief and gratitude. She smiled back at him.

"I've already called Tom to let him know the bad news and that you'll need to postpone your backpacking trip while we're in West Virginia for the funeral."

Memories of his grandfather filled the hours in flight, instead of the much-needed sleep Will hoped to get. Ann was restless, as well.

"You need to try to nap if you can," she said. "Tomorrow's going to be a long day."

"I just keep thinking about how much he shaped my life. When Grandpa started getting up in years, he lost some of his dexterity and found it difficult to shave. I would go to his house and give him the whole barbershop treatment. Every time a shave was completed, he would say without fail, 'Thank you 'til you're better paid.' Ann, that man taught me to be a kind and considerate gentleman, just like him. How am I supposed to bury him? How do I let him go?" Will looked searchingly at Ann for answers.

"You don't let go. You never let go. He'll always be with you. I see him every day in your eyes."

Will loved so many things about Ann, and at that moment, his appreciation for her support and heartfelt words was boundless. All he could do was reach over and hold her hand, thinking how lucky he was to have her to walk through this sadness with him.

The plane landed, and the couple made their way to Will's grandparents' house, which was about 35 minutes from the airport. Everything seemed so familiar to Will, yet so different at the same time. He had traveled these roads for years visiting his grandparents, but this time the scenery looked dark, as though a shadow of death and deep loss blanketed the land with sadness.

The historic two-story home, reminiscent of an 1850's railroad stop, had a stark-white expansive front porch, upon which sat six oak rocking chairs. Many summer nights were spent there on the threshold of Will's youth. He would listen to his grandparents, as they sat rocking with neighbors, talking about World War II, the plight of farmers, coal mining, and whoever happened to be the latest bootlegger to get caught selling moonshine. So many memories live on that porch.

As the rental car made its way up the drive, and the house came into full view, Will saw his grandmother standing on the porch, as if she'd been there all night waiting for her husband to come home. Will slowly got out of the car and started towards her. He couldn't help but notice that she seemed years older than when he visited last month. When he reached the top of the steps, he embraced his strong, independent grandmother, as she melted into his arms.

Very few times had Will ever witnessed her display emotions with such abandon, and it took only a few moments before he was sobbing with her.

Ann walked up and reached out, rubbing the old woman's back in a gesture of comfort.

"I'm so sorry about Jerry. He was a wonderful man, Emma."

"Thank you, dear. I'm so glad you and Billy are here."

Still at a loss for words to convey his feelings, Will pulled his head back a bit and looked into his grandmother's eyes for some kind of reassurance, which she sensed.

"It's going to be okay," she said. "Your grandfather loved you so much."

"I'm so sorry I wasn't here to say goodbye."

"Billy, you were in your grandfather's thoughts to the very end."

After another few moments of embrace, they made their way into the house. Will had always considered his grandparent's living room to be a shrine of sorts. It was in the center of the house, like a Great Hall, and all visiting and singing took place there. It was where laughter and tears, deep conversations and small talk, celebrations, and Sunday afternoon naps occurred, and today was no exception. Neighbors, friends, and family had already started to gather to grieve with Will's grandmother and to share memories of his grandfather, Jerry Harvey.

"Lou, you remember when Jerry and Emma would break out their guitar and banjo? Damn, if I could ever figure how he got his harmonica strapped to his banjo, so he could play both of them at the same time," one man said.

"Sure do remember," said Lou, a blond-haired, heavy-set lady sitting on the sofa, facing the fireplace. "Emma and Jerry always had a house full. Their parties are legendary."

Just as the statement left her mouth, Lou noticed that Will and his grandmother were standing just inside the front door, listening to them talk.

"Sorry, Emma, we were just remembering stories about Jerry."

"It's nice to hear how much he's remembered."

"It's the singing that I remember the most," Will's sister-in-law, Sally said, as she came in from the kitchen to set a tray of Emma's famous cheese biscuits on the coffee table.

Will chimed in, almost interrupting Sally, "Yeah, those were great sing-ins, but the very best part of the whole show, at least for me, was the trick Granddad got his dog, Karo, to do. I enjoyed all of them, but, the best one was when Granddad said, 'Karo, would you rather be married or dead?' Karo would roll over on his side, close his eyes, and play dead. That funny, little dog would do it perfectly every time," Will said. He could feel his emotions growing stronger by talking about his grandpa.

Lou broke the silence, "Jerry and Karo weren't the only characters around this house. I remember a Christmas trip to the emergency room by one Ms. Emma."

Folks started nodding their heads in agreement, and even Will laughed for the first time since getting the news about his grandpa. The story was well-known by all.

"It's your story, Emma, so why don't you tell it again?" Lou said.

"No, go ahead, you're doing fine. You tell it."

Lou said, "Okay, you asked for it. It seems that Emma and Jerry were just married and decorating their first Christmas tree.

Emma took notice of Jerry on his hands and knees looking under the tree with his behind being the only thing of him that could be seen. It was an opportunity Emma just couldn't resist. So with careful aim, she landed a swift kick with her bare foot, right on target. Jerry's derriere came out fine, but Emma got a broken big toe."

A solid round of laughter and applause followed the wonderful story of a happy couple.

Will's grandmother's laughter soon turned to noticeable sadness. The stories told were meant to comfort, as best they could, but they began to take a toll on her. It was like being at one of their great parties from the past, except the star was missing. Will was certain that if his grandpa was watching, he would approve with wholehearted laughter at the stories.

The following day, Jeremy Harvey was laid to rest with full military honors, a service properly befitting a World War II Veteran and member of the "Greatest Generation." So many people spoke about how he served his country with bravery and courage, how he raised his family with honor and dignity, and how he nurtured his friendships with care and tenacity. Surely, no one will ever be able to fill this man's shoes, especially for Will.

After the funeral, a great many people gathered at the house to pay their last respects. Finally, one lady simply said to Will's grandmother, "Jerry will be sorely missed." And with that, it was all over and done with. The time was now upon those who loved him most to learn how to live without him in their lives. The real work in losing someone never begins until everyone else has gone home and back to living their normal lives.

||

CHAPTER THREE
Letters from Grandfather

Right after lunch and a brief nap for Will's grandmother, she came out to sit with Will and Ann on the front porch. Ann was right; the day had been both long and tough, but it was perfectly beautiful in its own special way.

"Billy, I have a chore to perform that involves you. Are you ready?"

"Of course, Grandmother, how can I help?" Will replied.

"Well, it's a promise I made to your grandfather when he returned from World War II. He showed me a small metal box, which was locked. A key was tied to it with a bright red ribbon. He said to me, 'Emma, I have something in this box that I don't want you to see until I'm gone. When that time comes, you'll learn why, and you'll understand, alright?' I asked him why he couldn't tell me, and he simply said I'd understand. He insisted I keep my promise to wait. So I did.

"In 1977, he added a letter to the box addressed to you, our 16-year-old grandson. He also asked that upon his death, the box be opened by you. Your grandfather shared that letter with me prior to placing it in the box. So, here you are, Billy. Now I want to see what secret that box contains that was so important to your grandfather."

Ann said, "Open it up, Billy, the honor's all yours."

With trembling hands, Will carefully opened the box, as his grandmother and wife leaned forward for a closer view. The letter addressed to him was right on top. Knowing that this letter didn't contain the secret his grandmother had waited to learn for so long, Will set it aside and continued to take the other items from the box.

Surprisingly, there were none of the usual things one might expect from a veteran returning from war. There were no souvenirs—flags, guns, or knives. But, there were some items that caught Will's attention—maps and sketches of the area around Dutch Harbor, Alaska that were used in 1942 by the US Air Force personnel in WWII. Will's first thoughts went to his friend, Tom, who he knew would find them interesting because of the amount of reading he had done on the war.

Next, Will picked up an aged, brown envelope that was addressed, 'To Emma.'

Ann said, "That's got to be it—the one with the secret!"

"Would you like to read it, Grandmother," Will asked thoughtfully.

"No, you read it, dear; I would rather hear it through you."

Will carefully opened the envelope to reveal a letter, dated June 3, 1942. He could hear his grandfather's voice distinctly in the words written.

This letter is a documentation of my experience in Alaska in case I do not survive the coming battle at Dutch Harbor. We have broken the Japanese radio code, so we know of their plans to attack the harbor today.

We anticipate the unfortunate possibility that when they invade the harbor, the Japanese will capture us all as prisoners of war. So, we met last night in the mess hall and wrote our last wills and testaments. It was then that we also agreed to make a pact to commit suicide, rather than allow ourselves to be captured. We know of the cruel treatment that POWs receive at the hands of the Japanese, and we refuse to

*give them that satisfaction or suffer their
brutality. We will not become POWs.*

*I hope with all my heart that I will be
lucky enough to come home to you, my darling
Emma, after the war is over.*

> *With all my love,*
> *Jerry*

Will's grandmother sat in shocked silence for a few moments before she said, "Thank God, Jerry *was* lucky and *did* come home. I wish I could've heard about the secret pact directly from him. It would have been alright. I think it's sadder for me to learn it this way. But, just think how lucky we were to have him come home safely."

They all agreed on that.

Ann said, "Okay Will, now we want to hear what your grandfather had to say to you. It's not about the war because it was written in 1977."

Will picked up the letter, not knowing what to expect from his grandfather. On the front of the envelope, a handwritten post-it-note was dated June of 1990. The letter read:

*Billy, this is a copy of the letter I gave
you in 1977, which we discussed at length about
some ideas and personal philosophies you should
utilize to lead you to develop your own
guidelines for a quality life.*

*You were just 16 years old then. I believe
you will remember the discussion, but I
seriously doubt that you remember much about
the specific philosophies or even where your
copy of the letter is now. So, I've placed a
copy of it in this box for you.*

Now that you are an adult, the whole letter will make more sense to you.

Grandpa

"Oh! I remember that letter," exclaimed Will. "And, I remember the conversation, alright. But, I don't remember much of what I read or heard from grandpa. In fact, much of what I did hear, I didn't understand. He was right about that. And, of course, I have no idea what happened to the original letter."

"Will, for goodness sake. You were only 16 years old. Of course, you don't remember much of anything about it. But, what a thoughtful idea of your grandfather to think of this and save a copy for you," said Ann. "He must have felt it was very important information for you to have."

"That was your grandfather. Now let's hear the letter," said Grandmother.

Will opened the envelope and began to read:

June 1977

Dear Billy,

I just want you to know that I think you are one terrific young man at age 16. You are smart, with a pleasing personality. You are courteous, well-mannered, and easy going. You are also very respectful, a characteristic that I value highly. So, it is no wonder that I think you have what it takes to become very successful in whatever career you choose.

Now, at the risk of sounding like I am preaching, I want to share with you some practical ideas I have used all my life, and that I wish I had learned at an early age. I plan to see you soon, and we can talk about all this, man-to-man. So, jot down any questions you might have. Also, I suggest that you keep this letter in a safe place. You never know when you might feel the need to refer to it.

Some of the following things you already know, but they bear repeating:

1. Persistence is the cornerstone of success. My father called it 'stick-to-it-ness.' Don't give up. Don't ever give up.

2. The fear of failure can be crippling. We all fail sometimes. But, that's okay. Just don't be afraid to try.

3. The fear of going too far can often keep you from going as far as you can. Set your goals carefully, and go for them with gusto!

Remember that you and I will continue to have a special bond that even death cannot penetrate.

I love you and best wishes for a wonderful life.

Love, Grandpa

After reading this letter, there wasn't a dry eye between them. *I am going to see my grandmother more often than I did in the past and remember to tell her what she means to me, while she is still alive to hear it,* Will promised himself.

On their flight home, Will held his grandpa's box in his lap, unwilling to surrender it to the airline attendant or the luggage handlers. To him, the box held his grandfather's memory and everything he meant to him. Will glanced over at Ann, who was flipping through the pages of a magazine.

"You okay?" Ann asked, as she felt Will look in her direction.

"Yeah, I'm okay. I was just thinking that I hope I can live to be half the man my grandfather was and to walk in his footsteps. He was a real gentleman."

"Yes, he was an amazing man—just like you," Ann said proudly.

‖

CHAPTER FOUR
Thank You 'til You're Better Paid

The airport taxi pulled up in front of the Sellers' home. The rain had been unrelenting since they landed in Richmond. Ann and Will jumped from the cab and hurried to their front porch. Besides the grass growing tall from the heavy showers, everything looked fairly normal—except the porch and living room lights were on.

"Ann, surely we didn't leave those lights on the whole time we were in West Virginia, did we?"

"No, of course not," replied Ann. "We never do that. It can't be burglars because they don't turn lights on. Oh, I know! Michele! I bet it was Michele. She turned the lights on for us. Doesn't that seem like something she would do?"

The taxi driver placed their luggage on the front porch and left, as Will and Ann turned the key in the lock on the front door of their home and entered the foyer. The lights were on in the kitchen, too. Right away, they noticed how clean-smelling and beautiful the house looked—far better than the way they left it when they rushed out to the airport a few days ago.

Fresh-cut flowers graced the living room coffee table. They knew instantly that Michele and Tom were the thoughtful culprits and welcome-home committee. The smell of fresh-brewed coffee beckoned them from the kitchen, as the couple hung up their wet coats and followed the inviting aroma.

"Will, look—we have a whole pot of hot coffee!" exclaimed Ann. "Here's a note from Michele on the kitchen cabinet."

Welcome home guys!
Sorry about your grandfather, Will.
Tom and I wanted to do something extra-special for
you, so we had your entire house thoroughly cleaned.
We hope you like it (and hope you wiped your feet at
the front door!).
  Coffee is on. Pizza and beer are in the fridge.

Love,
Michele

P.S. If you're not too tired tonight, Tom and I will
come over and share the pizza and beer with you. Let
us know.

Will called right away, and Tom answered, "I've been waiting for your call. We'll be right over."

"What wonderful friends we have in Michele and Tom. We owe them one," said Ann.

Just then, their 'no-need-to-knock' friends walked into the kitchen, and the couples caught up over pizza and beer.

"You two are the greatest," said Will. "Thank you 'til you're better paid," he added. "How's that for a grandpa-ism?"

"What's a grandpa-ism?" Michele asked.

"Think of it as a bit of wisdom from my grandfather. He had lots of them. Here's one that could apply to friends, like us, 'There are few problems that cannot be solved if you keep talking about them in an open and positive way.'"

"I hope it never comes to that between us, but if it does, I'll remember that grandpa-ism. Your grandfather sounds like he was very wise."

"Speaking of Grandfather, I have something I know you're going to find interesting, Tom. It's a box of things he wanted me to have. Much of it is related to his experience as a sergeant in the Air Force in the battle of Dutch Harbor, Alaska during

WWII. Maybe tomorrow, after we're more rested, you and Michele can come back over, and you and I'll go through it."

With that, Will signaled a close to the night's visit, "Until then, Tom, would you mind if I hugged your wife goodnight?"

"Not if I can hug yours," his friend quickly replied. "Have a good night, you two."

As soon as they left, Will said wistfully, "Well, sweetheart, here we are in our perfectly pristine home with nothing to do but go to bed—any ideas come to mind…besides sleep?"

Ann said, "I have an idea. Fix us a brandy, and make mine a double. I'll be upstairs. I think you'll like what I have in mind."

Will happily poured the brandies, turned off all the lights, locked the doors, tidied up the kitchen, and headed upstairs to see what his wife had on her mind. He was sure she'd given him 'the look,' and he knew what that meant.

When Will got to their bedroom, with brandy in hand and joyful expectation in his heart, he found his beautiful and supportive wife had slipped into his favorite red negligee and lit candles all around their bedroom. It was quite the romantic scene, except…Will found his special 'love-devil' fast asleep on the bed.

The last few days of hustle and bustle, with enough raw emotions to last for weeks, had finally caught up with Ann. Smiling at the sweet sight of his lovely wife and all her good intentions, Will knew there would be plenty of time for brandy tomorrow night and far more sparks of energy between them. So, being the caring husband that he was, Will put the glasses of brandy by the bedside, blew out the candles, and snuggled up tightly to his devilishly-wonderful wife.

The next morning seemed to come quickly as Tom and Michele showed up early at the Sellers' home. Tom was, indeed, most anxious to see the WWII mementos left to Will by his grandfather, and Will was all-too-happy to share his treasures.

He ran upstairs to retrieve the box from the closet while Tom eagerly waited in the living room.

"I just can't believe we never talked about your grandfather serving at Dutch Harbor during WWII. Do you realize how important the Battles of Midway and Dutch Harbor were to America winning the war?"

Will knew his friend was a World War II buff. "Not really, Tom. Granddad and I never talked about the war that much. In fact, I just found out something really big that even Grandmother didn't know. Prior to the Dutch Harbor invasion, Grandfather and his fellow airmen made a secret pact to commit suicide before they'd allow themselves to be taken as POWs by the Japanese."

"No kidding? That's incredible!" exclaimed Tom.

"He wrote about it in a letter to Grandmother that was to be read by me, only after his death."

The excitement was almost more than Tom could take. "Wow! How amazing was that?"

"Yeah, it was. You want to tell me what you know about Dutch Harbor before we go through the box?" Will asked.

"Okay, sure. I actually know quite a bit about it; that's why I am so interested in what your grandfather left you. First, it's important to know that the battle, which is remembered in history as the Battle of Midway, came six months after Pearl Harbor—and we all know how that went. So, the success at Midway is what many historians consider to be the turning point in the war.

"It was there that American forces finally succeeded in breaking through the strength of the Japanese Navy, due mainly to two major events: The first was when US radio operators broke the enemy code without the Japanese ever realizing their messages were being intercepted. And the second major event occurred when we received information about an impending attack on Dutch Harbor. The enemy's plan was to divide and weaken the US troops at Midway by forcing them to split up and defend a separate attack on Alaska. But because of the advance notice, our forces didn't fall for this diversionary tactic and kept most of our efforts at Midway, where they were most needed.

"Another factor that played a key role in the American success was a dense fog at 4 a.m. on June 3, 1942 at Dutch Harbor. The weather caused one of the two Japanese Zero Aircraft carriers, the JUNYO, which was headed for Alaska, to withdraw from battle.

"So, the damage to Dutch Harbor was relatively insignificant. The greatest surprise to the Japanese was the American response to the attack on Dutch Harbor—how we were battle-ready for both of the invasions. It wasn't the surprise the Japanese intended."

"Wow! I see why you are so interested in the war—you really know your stuff," Will said. "You are like a walking WWII encyclopedia. Why the heck don't you teach History somewhere instead of crunching numbers for a living?"

"Who knows?" answered Tom.

Going through Will's box of memories from the Battle of Dutch Harbor, Tom seemed lost in thought. Suddenly, he stopped, and without a word, stared blankly into space. Then, he turned to face Will with his eyes opened wide in a classic aha-moment look.

"Will! Why don't we forget about hiking the Appalachian Trail and go backpacking at Dutch Harbor! Just think—we can hike the same trails that your grandfather did in 1942! Wouldn't that be something—exactly fifty years later?"

"You're serious? Go all the way to Dutch Harbor, Alaska?"

"You're damned right, that's precisely what I mean! It could be the adventure of a lifetime!"

Will sat stunned, staring at Tom, but thinking that the idea might be right on time. What a thrill it would be to actually walk in his grandfather's footsteps during such a historic anniversary.

After a few minutes of silence, Tom said, "Why not? Let's go for it—what do you say? Let's go back in time for the chance to experience a little bit of life as members of the 'Greatest Generation,' if only for a brief moment!"

Will was still playing with the notion in his mind.

"Okay, if you're really serious—I'm in!"

"Terrific!" said Tom, with uncontained excitement. "It'll be a real WWII adventure."

"Yeah, we can even pretend that we're young men in the USA Air Force assigned to my grandfather's company as radio operators in Dutch Harbor."

Snapping back to reality, they both laughed and headed off to the kitchen to see if their wives would be onboard with their change of plans.

"Are you kidding? Of course, Michele and I can entertain ourselves while you're gone, can't we, Michele?"

"Yep, we'll shop 'til we drop, as the saying goes. And then, we'll get up and shop 'til we drop some more," the women laughed.

The idea, born as an aha moment for one and inspiring a childlike moment of pretend-play for the other, appeared to be quickly turning into a plan of real adventure for two 30-year-old friends on a mission to add some spice to their lives. Soon, they would be off to the mountains of Alaska for a backpacking trip filled with some unexpected reminders of World War II.

||

CHAPTER FIVE
Next Stop—Dutch Harbor, Alaska

Will found his grandfather's passing so close to the 50-year anniversary of the Battle at Dutch Harbor rather serendipitous. He knew his grandfather would be extremely touched and proud that his grandson wanted to walk in his footsteps during that historic WWII battle. Will thought, *Maybe Grandfather will manage to be there with us in spirit. Who could say?*

Tom and Will wanted to be in Dutch Harbor as close to the actual date of the battle as possible. Perhaps that would help them feel the special energy of the day. Their plane was set to land on June 2, 1992, which would allow them to be hiking in the mountains the next day, the exact date of the battle —June 3, 1942.

Alaskan weather can be pretty disagreeable any time of the year with fog, rain, and wind. The men were hoping they might get lucky with their first backpacking excursion and hit a decent spell of weather.

The flight was long and tiring, with stops in Chicago, Seattle, and Anchorage—until finally, the captain of the plane announced, "Ladies and Gentlemen, we will be arriving momentarily at our destination of Dutch Harbor, in the Aleutian chain of Alaska. The weather forecast is predicting warmer than usual temperatures for the next few days—a balmy 55 degrees with clear skies, but it looks like we'll have a foggy landing today. Thank you for flying with us. Our entire flight crew hopes you have a memorable stay in Alaska."

Tom was about to come out of his skin with excitement. Will, just off his recent trip to West Virginia, was looking most forward to putting his feet on solid ground for a while.

"Thank God, we're here, said Will."

"Man, the weather's going to be perfect. This is going to be so great! Everything's going our way, exclaimed Tom."

To characterize Dutch Harbor as isolated would be an understatement. It's a small town on a harbor with large fields of colorful flowers in the spring and summer. The ancient volcanic mountains could not be missed, usually with snow on their caps. One thing, about the landscape that grabbed the men's attention was the absence of trees. Virginia is a tree mecca, but because the mountains of Alaska consist mainly of volcanic rock, formed from hot larva, trees were an uncommon sight.

On the plane's final approach to the Dutch Harbor airport, the fog was all that could be seen from the windows—thick, impenetrable fog. The plane continued to descend at reduced speed until suddenly it broke under the soup, and visibility appeared like magic. The landing was as smooth as silk.

"That's what used to be called a three-point landing," Will said.

"I am thinking that means it was good. I am sure pilots who fly in and out of Alaska are used to challenging landings, Tom replied."

A fellow passenger, sitting nearby added, "That landing was normal for this part of the country. Wait until you have to land in an Alaskan storm. That will scare your socks off."

"I am hoping *not* to have that pleasure, thank you," Will said, smiling back at the gentleman.

They taxied to the terminal, which was the smallest airport terminal either of the men had ever experienced.

"I thought Richmond's airport was small, Will said.

"Wow! Can you believe it? We are actually in Alaska," said Tom.

As they entered the terminal's waiting room, which was accordingly small, there to greet them was a rather pretty volunteer, representing the town.

"Welcome to Dutch Harbor. My name is Sue. I'm Dutch Harbor's welcoming committee. Actually, it's not a real *committee*, she smiled. It consists of one person, and I'm it."

Singling them out as visitors in need of more attention, as most of the other passengers appeared to be regulars, Sue asked, "Tell me, what brings you fellas' to Dutch Harbor, and how I can be of assistance?"

"Hello, Sue. I'm Will, and this is my good friend, Tom. We're here from Richmond, Virginia, to do some backpacking. Can you guide us to someone with information about the area, specifically to hiking trails in the mountains and anything else in terms of weather and unusual sights?"

She said, "Sure, okay." With a warm smile, she added, "I can tell from your accents that you are Southern gentlemen. I'll be happy to recommend someone who'll be very pleased to help you. Have a seat right over there, and give me a few minutes. I'll be right back."

As Sue attended to a few more visitors, Tom and Will went to claim their backpacking gear before returning to wait for Sue. She was back in about five minutes, and they picked up the conversation where it left off.

She said, with obvious pleasure, "I know just the person for you to see. Her name is Mildred Johnson. Mildred owns and operates the Southern Bakery at 110 Main Street. It's called the Southern Bakery for a reason; she's a Southerner, too—from North Carolina, I think. Mildred's one of the most popular people in town, and she keeps us all well-fed on those Southern biscuits they make from scratch every day. I know she'll be so glad to see y'all," she exclaimed with a wink, placing great emphasis on y'*all*.

Tom just couldn't resist some exaggerated Southern drawl, "Well, bless my soul, and thanky, ma'am."

The three of them laughed so loudly that everyone in the room looked up to see what was so funny.

"Say, you two gentlemen are so friendly. If you have time, let's get together. I'd love to hear more about life in the South. I'm at the police station when I'm not volunteering here." And, in her best Southern accent, Sue said, "Y'all come back now, ya hear? Don't forget to tell Mildred that Sue sent you."

"Man, I already like Alaska," said Will, as they departed for Main Street. Both men felt they had received extra-special attention and were very pleased that such a warm welcome was given to strangers.

Sue's directions to the bakery were easy to follow, and they found it without any problem. Exuding a sense of Southern charm and hospitality, the small bakery was very welcoming with bright paint colors and warm lighting. As soon as they entered the front door, they felt a sense of home.

A friendly young lady wearing a white apron approached them immediately. "I bet you are Tom and Will—the Southern gentlemen. Sue called a few minutes ago; I'm Sylvia," she said.

"Wow, news travels fast in Alaska, and yes, you would be correct, I am Will, and this is Tom."

Just then, the kitchen door swung open, and the men got a wonderful whiff of the delicious-smelling Southern biscuits Sue told them about. Will was taken straight back to his childhood when his mother baked homemade biscuits with the same aroma.

Sylvia noticed their pleasure and said, "That's the smell of our Southern-style cheese biscuits; they're our specialty. Sit anywhere you want, and I'll bring you some straight from the oven. Would you like coffee?"

Both men nodded, "Yes, please."

Sylvia returned right away with the coffee. "Mildred will be out in just a minute," she said.

Mildred was quite a surprise, particularly to Will, who expected to see a middle-aged woman dressed in blue jeans, flannel shirt, and some waterproof tundra boots like those on models in an L.L. Bean catalog. What he saw was a gorgeous blue-eyed blond with a school-girl figure.

Mildred was, undoubtedly, the sweetheart of Dutch Harbor. Her hair was arranged in a neat ponytail, and her makeup was expertly applied like on the faces of models in beauty magazines. As she engaged in conversation with Will and Tom, her warm personality and charm only enhanced her appearance. Will didn't expect to find the epitome of a Southern lady, with such grace and beauty, in the Alaskan wilderness.

"I can hardly believe there are people from Virginia in my bakery," Mildred said, longingly. "Just seeing you two gentlemen makes me homesick for the South. I'm from North Carolina, originally, but this has been my home for many years, and I really like it here. Welcome to Alaska."

"We've been here such a short time, and already we've met three people who are gracious and friendly to a fault," Will said. "Is everybody here like you, Sue, and Sylvia?"

"Well, no. Not everyone, at least, not in the beginning. Some have a suspicious, standoffish attitude when they meet a stranger. Some call it the Alaskan mindset, but eventually, most come around."

The biscuits arrived with more coffee, and Will and Tom dove right in.

Then Mildred asked, "Now, what's this I hear about you two wanting to hike in our mountains? Day hiking is one thing, but backpacking?"

Will explained to her about his grandfather serving in the Air Force during the battle of Dutch Harbor.

"We're anxious to do some backpacking, and we decided that instead of the Blue Ridge Mountains in Virginia, we wanted to follow in the footsteps of my grandfather, while also pursuing a great adventure."

"Are you serious?" Mildred appeared surprised. "Have you done any research into what kind of mountains we have here? They are nothing like the Blue Ridge Mountains. These mountains are made of volcanic rock! There are a few trails, but they don't reach far into the mountains. And, there are no trees, so no fuel for campfires. I just don't think you will like backpacking here. I certainly don't recommend it; day hiking maybe, but backpacking—that's a whole different bear."

Will and Tom listened intently with curiosity at the great effort Mildred was making to discourage two strangers from exploring some trails in Dutch Harbor. Both of them thought she was way out of line in assuming they wouldn't be able to handle the terrain, without knowing anything about them.

"She even threw a bear into the picture," Tom said, after she walked away. "I could've done without that."

"By the way," said a voice from the back of the bakery, "I want to thank the grandson of a man who helped defend our town against the Japanese in WWII. All those servicemen are our heroes."

The voice belonged to a young man named Harold, who was employed as a cook at the bakery.

"Mildred, I couldn't help but overhear your conversation," said Harold. "Maybe these two gentlemen would be interested in seeing the area in back of us that was used as a relay radio station in 1942. You know the place. It might be a perfect spot for them to make their first camp. I'd be glad to guide them up there. It isn't very far, and I could be back at work in no time. That could be their base campsite to explore the area a bit and then judge for themselves whether to pursue things further up here."

"Why, thank you, Harold," said Tom. "That's a great idea!"

"Yes, that sounds perfect, if it isn't too much bother," Will agreed.

Before they left the bakery with Harold, a beautiful young girl with long black hair and large brown eyes appeared out of nowhere. She appeared to be in her early teens.

"You are Will and Tom, aren't you?" the girl said, without a moment's hesitation.

"That's right," said Will, as both men nodded in agreement. But before they could say another word, the personable young lady continued talking to them.

"I'm Josephine, but folks around here call me JoJo. I'm Mildred's daughter. I think you've already met my mom, haven't you?"

"Yes, we have. It's nice to meet you, Miss Johnson," said Tom.

"Oh, my last name isn't Johnson. Everybody thinks it is, but it's not. I usually don't bother correcting anyone; I just let them think Johnson's my last name, like my mom's."

Tom's curiosity was piqued, "Well, if it isn't Johnson, then, what is your name?"

"It's Nakamoto. I have other nicknames. Would you like to hear them?"

"I really like JoJo," Will told the girl. "It seems to fit you to a tee, but sure, tell us the others."

"Okay, one is 'J3'—Get it? JoJo Johnson," she said with a giggle. "Mom says my last name's a secret, so don't tell anyone, okay?"

Harold interrupted the conversation by suggesting they'd better get going, so he could get back to work as soon as possible.

"Your secret's safe with us, JoJo," Will assured the girl as he and Tom told her goodbye. It seemed strange to the men that a child's last name would be a secret, but they had more pressing things to think about at the moment, so their curiosity faded.

Harold drove them to the parking lot that led to the trail up toward the mountain. Tom thought the first thing they should do when they arrived at the radio relay spot was to take another look at Will's granddad's maps to see if they could determine whether they were actually where he was in 1942.

"Tom, this trip was such a great idea. Thanks for suggesting we do it and for taking this long journey with me. I believe it could be the most meaningful trip I'll ever take," Will said, as he and his long-time friend and neighbor started up the mountain.

"Pleasure's all mine, man! I bet we'll both look back on this Alaskan adventure as something special. I just pray a grizzly doesn't try to add to the thrill of it all. That's an experience I want to avoid."

"That's for sure," said Harold.

Laughing in agreement, the men remembered to talk in very loud voices to lessen the possibility of any such excitement.

The trails close to the town of Dutch Harbor were easy to hike and featured beautiful scenery. With the rain stopped and the fog lifted, good views were visible of the entire landscape. Colorful flowers blazed large lush meadows, and an abundance of birds was in constant flight everywhere.

But, there it was—the oddity of it all—no trees. How strange to see such a beautiful place without trees. The men knew Mildred was right about one thing—there would be no campfires. However, recalling Andy's warnings about the danger of fires in windy conditions made Will and Tom realize that even if there were trees in these volcanic mountains, a campfire would have been risky because there always seemed to be a slight wind blowing in Alaska.

The trail was in good shape as they trudged along with Harold before finally arriving at the designated spot.

"Here it is!" Harold jubilantly exclaimed. He seemed proud that he had successfully put the Virginians onto the path of their

Alaskan adventure. Wishing them well, he quickly turned and disappeared back down the trail to the bakery.

Will and Tom got busy setting up camp. The tent was their main concern and no simple matter, especially with the wind picking up. Somehow, the new backpacking aficionados met with success. After a cold dinner that left little to the imagination and satisfaction, Will pulled out his granddad's maps. They were thrilled to find that, to the best of the two men's knowledge, they were, indeed, in the exact spot where Will's grandfather had walked.

With little else to do but dream of the exploration they would begin tomorrow, when two best friends planned to step back into history on the anniversary of the Battle of Dutch Harbor, they settled down inside their tent for the night. Perhaps they would dream that they were members of the 'Greatest Generation' and proud servicemen of the USA Air Force, defending the state of Alaska and the country against a Japanese invasion during WWII.

That is, if the flapping of the tent in the wind would permit them to fall asleep.

||

CHAPTER SIX
In the Event of a Bear Scare

Over a cold breakfast of dried fruit and trail mix, Tom and Will discussed a plan for the day. Based on what they had learned from Mildred, backpacking in Alaska may include some not-so-enjoyable challenges, mainly because of the conditions of the barren terrain in volcanic mountains. But it was too late to turn back now.

"We certainly can't even think about going home without checking the trails out enough to make a rational decision on our own—not after coming all this way, right?"

Tom, halfway laughing, replied, "Not if we ever want to hear the end of it; that's for sure. I just wish Mildred hadn't mentioned the 'b-word.' I think I even dreamed about one last night. Just the thought of an encounter with a grizzly makes my skin crawl—but, let's stop thinking the worst and get on with the adventure we came to have."

"Good idea, my friend. Besides, I thought Mildred was being overly discouraging, and who knows what that was about? Didn't you find it odd how she went on so passionately about the danger we were putting ourselves in? She doesn't know us well enough to care about what happens to us. Let's look around a bit, and decide for ourselves."

"I agree, but Will, we really don't have a plan for what we'd do in the event of a bear scare. This being so close to town and all, what do you think the chances are that we could run into one out here? We're only a couple of miles from town."

Will said, matter-of-factly, "I read in a visitor's guide that wherever you are in Alaska, you're never far from a bear. It also said it doesn't matter whether it's a brown grizzly or a black bear, they're all very dangerous, and every effort should be made to avoid an encounter with them. They confirmed what Andy told us about how Alaskan bears aren't like the black bears back in Virginia that just go into camps looking for food; the nature of an Alaskan bear is to actually attack people. I guess you didn't think about bears when you had your 'aha moment' of coming to Alaska, did you, buddy?"

"Obviously not, so we need to think now—what if we should run into one up here? We need a plan."

"Well, you remember what else Andy said, don't you? The main thing is *not* to run. Bears have poor eyesight, so when they see you, they may not be sure what you are. If you run, they might think you are food and chase you. So, we definitely don't run.

"Our biggest worry around here is probably the 'garbage bears' that stay close to towns and communities. They're always searching for food in garbage cans, and though they're less interested in eating people than garbage, they're still dangerous."

"This information is not helping my anxiety levels at all. If we do see one, let's hope he's full of garbage and not interested in adding us to the menu!"

"Yeah, let's hope. Oh, another thing. The State of Alaska recommends that if you hike in any areas outside of towns, you should be armed because people are being mauled by bears all the time. We have no gun; how bright is that?"

"If we keep talking about this, I may not care what our wives say if we come home early. Seriously, maybe we should head back to town and buy a couple of guns, just to be safe, before we tromp around very far out here."

"Maybe we should first decide if we are going to stay up here, and then see if we want to go back for guns or not. Let's calm down, check out the area today, and then make our decision."

"Okay, said Tom, still worried, "but we'd better not go very far into the mountains, just in case."

The radio station made for an almost perfect base campsite. There were no trees, of course, but there were some large rocks on the southwest border that proved invaluable for blocking the wind. The rocks could not block the rain, however, so when the men were ready to explore more of the trail, they left some of their gear and food inside the tent. According to the weather report by the plane's captain, rain was not expected, but the Alaskan weather was famous for harsh conditions coming without notice. The skies were overcast, but it was still a very pleasant day by local standards.

The first trail looked more like a path than a hiking trail. It was rather narrow and rocky, but it appeared to be in frequent use. Tom's first thought was that it might be a path used by animals. He tried to keep his mind off what type of animals, as he led the way in single file. Walking silently, the men were paying more attention to their feet on the path than their surroundings. Suddenly, Tom stopped dead in his tracks.

Before Will could ask him why he stopped, Tom turned his head slightly towards him, his eyes still looking forward, as he whispered, "*bear*," from the corner of his mouth.

The huge bear stood between seven and eight feet tall. Its coat was shaggy with long matted hair, and its sharp white teeth were beyond menacing. The beast emitted a low growl as saliva dripped from its open mouth. A foul odor filled the air in the 35 to 40 feet of distance between the animal and the men. Whether it was a brown or black bear seemed highly irrelevant at the moment; this bear appeared to be either very angry or very hungry—or both.

It was probably a good thing that there was nowhere to run because that is exactly what the two men instinctively wanted to do as they faced the scariest moment of their lives. With no trees to climb and few-to-zero options, the men did the only thing they could do—they stood motionless, as did the bear. It appeared to be doing precisely what the men had learned about the animal's nature. It looked to be sizing them up, as if wondering what they were. They could only hope the bear's vision was not good enough to see their bodies trembling in absolute fear for their lives.

After a long 30-second standoff that seemed to last an hour, Will felt closer than ever to a heart attack from shock. Suddenly and without notice, Tom began to yell at the top of his lungs, jumping up and down while waving his arms wildly. Quickly catching on after finding his breath, Will began to do the same. The commotion either scared or confused the bear because it reared up and gave a vicious, loud roar as it turned and took off with the speed of a racehorse. It was totally out of sight within three short seconds.

With Tom's greatest fear materialized, he announced without hesitation, "Let's get the hell out of here." He didn't have to say it twice. Not nearly as fast as the bear, both men high-tailed it in the direction of town. With no gun for protection, their only defense was adrenaline-fused fear and hope that they wouldn't run into the monstrous bear again while they were trying to reach safety.

Once they felt they were at a reasonable distance from danger, they slowed their pace to catch their breath.

"Well, that was damn scary," Will said. "I guess we can officially say we survived our first bear encounter, but frankly, once is enough for me."

"Hell yeah—I'm over Alaska."

Will added, "I don't have any idea how far away that bear is right now, but I suggest we get back to town as fast as our legs will take us."

"I'm right with ya," Tom agreed.

The two didn't stop until they were safe inside the Southern Bakery. When Mildred saw them, she could tell by their facial expressions that something had gone terribly wrong. She looked very concerned and started questioning them right away. Both men were as pale as white skin can be, and practically hyperventilating, as they recounted their run-in with the bear. Her response was measured as she told them how very lucky they were that the bear didn't charge them.

"Many hikers in Alaska aren't so lucky," Mildred reiterated her point. "Folks around here rarely venture out of town without a weapon for protection, and I see you two don't have a gun between you. You should think about that, and let this be an important lesson learned. People get mauled here a lot, and I can tell you right now, you don't want to be mauled by a bear."

"I think that point has been made abundantly clear," said Tom, who wasn't in any mood for a bear-safety lecture.

And then she asked the inevitable, "So, have you decided to give up on the idea of backpacking up here?"

Will quickly satisfied Mildred's curiosity, "Yes, we've come to the conclusion that taking your advice is a good idea. We called and got a departure time for later this evening. We're heading home. The bear encounter took its toll on both of us. One of the main things we wanted to do here was to find the exact place where my grandfather operated his radio station during the battle of Dutch Harbor, and thanks to Harold, we believe we found it. So, mission accomplished."

"Well, that's wonderful," Mildred said, sounding relieved. "I'm really glad you found the relay station. I must say it's been a pleasure having you gentlemen and your Southern manners around here, even though it was only for a short while. I am truly going to miss you."

"Before we go to the airport, could we get a few photos with you and JoJo in your Alaskan Southern-style bakery?" Will asked.

"Absolutely!"

Tom and Will took a few photos and were about to leave when JoJo said she'd like to walk with them to the airport.

"I wanted this chance to talk with you in private," JoJo said. "I kind of have a favor to ask, but I don't really know where to start."

"What is it, JoJo?" Will asked.

After a brief pause, the teen opened up to the two men.

"Okay, here's the thing—I don't really like Alaska. In fact, I hate it, but my mom doesn't know that. She thinks I love it here as much as she does, and for some reason, she wants to stay forever. There's some strange attraction for her to Dutch Harbor that doesn't make sense to me at all.

"Truthfully, I'd love to visit Richmond, and I was wondering if you'd invite my mom and me to visit you? It wouldn't have to be a long visit, just a short one. I've seen pictures of Virginia, and it's so beautiful. Since I'll soon be ready for college, I might like to consider going to one there, maybe in Richmond. I thought Mom might be willing to arrange visits to a few schools while we're there. Then, maybe she'll remember how nice it is in the South and want to go back there to live."

Will replied, "JoJo, I'm sure that won't be a problem at all. Tom and I just need to talk to our wives to make arrangements, but I'm sure we'd all love to have you and your mom visit us. Then we can show you both some real Southern hospitality."

They arrived at the airport, and Sue was there. She seemed disappointed that their visit was cut short before they could get together, but she was a good sport and fully understood their reasoning after such a frightening experience with a bear.

She agreed to pictures with her new Southern friends. Will was especially excited about one he took of Sue hugging Tom. He couldn't wait to show it to Michele. He could hear himself joking that it was Tom's only *bear-hug* on the trip. That was sure to get Tom's goat and a big laugh from their wives. Will was barely able to contain his desire to laugh out loud with thoughts of his plan.

The two friends settled down in some soft chairs for a long wait until departure. It seemed like a perfect opportunity to catch a little shut-eye, since their emotionally-draining morning had followed a somewhat sleepless night in the tent.

||

CHAPTER SEVEN
A Last Hike to Remember

Will nodded off fairly easily in the small waiting room of the airport, where it was an unusually quiet day. Tom settled in with some reading materials but quickly became bored. After a short nap, Will woke up and saw that Tom was wide awake.

"It's only 10 a.m., and our plane doesn't leave until 6'oclock," said Will. "That's like sitting here for an entire workday. I can't sit here that long. What do you think about going back to the relay station and getting the stuff we left after that bear scared the bejesus out of us? There's more than enough time. Besides, there's no rain or fog, and the temperature's very comfortable."

Tom thought about the idea for a second or two. "That bear must not have scared you as much as me. I know it's not that far, but I'm still a little worried about that damn bear roaming around. Maybe we should just thank our lucky stars and let well enough be. There might even be bears at our campsite for the food we left in the tent. Did you think about that?"

"It crossed my mind, but even so, I think we'll be safe that close to town. We'll make a lot of noise going up the trail to chase away any bears. It worked for us before—thanks to you. Anyway, I thought you were the fearless outdoorsman between the two of us?"

"That was before Big Foot showed up. Fine, let's go do it. It shouldn't take us that long." Then regaining his manly composure, Tom added with a large grin, "I'll take care of you, wimp."

"That's more like it," Will smiled.

So off they went up the trail for one last hike. As they neared the campsite, the men began to sing robustly, 'Row, row, row your boat,' making as much noise as possible. The food packages were still just as they had left them. They performed a miraculous job of folding up the massive tent and inserting it in their backpack like they had been taught to do. But, they wisely opted to leave the few food items, so as not to draw the attention of bears. They both agreed it would be preferable for bears to be attracted to the campsite instead of to them.

Before leaving the radio relay station, they took a few moments to try and imagine how the scene may have looked with a radio shack there in 1942. It was emotional for Will to realize he was likely standing where his granddad had stood some 50 years earlier. Not wanting to linger any longer, they felt it was time to move out of there and head back to the airport. But after only a short walk, Tom had gathered up a new batch of courage and surprised Will with a brave thought.

"You know, the weather really is nice, and there's no sign of any wildlife," said Tom, purposefully steering clear of the mention of bears. "So, maybe we should go a little farther for exercise and take in more of the scenery before we leave for Richmond. After all, we don't get to this part of the country much, and we're still facing a long wait in that little room."

Will looked at Tom in disbelief and said, "Yeah, but there are no bears in that little room. Did you think of that? Also, remember, we still have no gun. You really want to take another chance out here?"

"Yep, I got my nerve back. I ain't afraid of no bears," Tom said, as he began singing the Ghostbusters' theme song.

"I never thought I'd hear you say that. You might be crazy, but at least you regained your sense of humor. Seriously though, let's be extremely careful. I really do want to get home in one piece—and I don't mean one *mangled* piece, either."

"We'll be fine. We'll stay close to town and on high alert the whole time."

The friends began their second final walk up the now-familiar trail for one more attempt at hiking in Alaska. Thinking a new trail they hadn't seen before would be more interesting, they soon found one that led around an outcropping of rock, which looked rather foreboding.

Though the new trail was isolated, it too, looked more worn by foot traffic than one would expect. The men finally came to a very steep and narrow path that descended into a deep ravine. They decided to take a look down into it from over the rim.

That's when confusion set in. About 50 yards into the ravine, there sat the impossible. Both men saw it, and neither said a word for what seemed like minutes. They were, at once, speechless. They blinked their eyes to try and readjust their focus into the distance for a reality that made sense to them.

"What the hell?" were the only words Will could finally stammer out, with no response from Tom, who was still too dumbstruck to speak.

The airplane sat upright and appeared to be in fairly good condition, considering it wasn't just *any* airplane, but a *World War II Zero fighter plane*. Coming to grips with what they saw before them, the men began moving down the narrow path toward what they couldn't yet believe. The WWII fighter looked to be complete with machine guns in the wings!

The weird reality began to set in with Tom, who had yet to utter a single word before he exclaimed, "*My God*, it's a propeller-driven Jap Zero—just like those used in the attack on Dutch Harbor in 1942! Look at that thing. How could it possibly be here?"

"It can't be real," said Will. "It must be a restored replica that someone crashed here recently…but, it's in astonishingly good condition for a crash in this rugged terrain. Even the canopy is unbroken. Maybe we should make sure there's not a dead or injured pilot in there."

As the men moved in for a closer look at their incredulous find, Tom raised a good question, "If these machine guns are as real as they look, that would make them illegal, right?"

"Yeah, as far as I know, those guns wouldn't be permitted even as a restoration. And at any rate, with machine guns still intact, the authorities of Dutch Harbor would have certainly removed this plane, don't you think?"

"If they know about it," Tom wonders aloud. "But, somebody must know about it, unless that was a highly-used bear path we were just on. Something or someone has been walking that path quite often, and it leads straight to this plane. Somehow, I doubt bears would have any interest in it unless there's food onboard—human or otherwise."

As they stood in their disbelief and confusion in front of the warplane, rustling noises stirred from behind it. Afraid it might be another bear, both men instantly froze in their tracks.

Suddenly, they were alarmed by the sound of a voice coming from behind the plane. Someone was speaking to them in a loud, harsh tone, but in a language neither of them understood.

"Maybe it's the pilot. Who's there? Where are you?" Tom yelled.

Again, the male voice rang out. Strangely, it sounded as though he was speaking Japanese, or could that be their minds playing tricks on them? Then, without warning, a man appeared. As he came quickly toward them, they could see that he was, indeed, Japanese, and he was outfitted in a military flight uniform. The men now found the whole scene even more bizarre, as they searched their minds for a reasonable explanation.

Finally, Tom spoke up, "Hey, are you alright, mister? Did you have an accident on the way to a WWII reenactment or something?"

The man continued to sound like he was barking orders at them. As though he finally realized that they could not comprehend his words, he motioned for them to put their hands up and sit down. Tom and Will tentatively followed his orders, though not knowing why they should do as he said.

Taking a small book from his pocket, the man referred to it for a few minutes before he started asking questions in broken English.

Tom said to Will, half under his breath but loud enough to be heard, "This guy is crazy or the biggest bozo in the world."

"I heard that," said the pilot, smugly, in near-perfect English. "Yes, I speak and understand English," he said, proudly enjoying their look of surprise.

"Then why did you pretend not to be able to speak our language?" asked Tom. "Are we being robbed by someone who also pretends to be a Japanese pilot? What do you want?"

"I speak English, and I understand your American culture. My sister and her husband are naturalized American citizens. They live in Los Angeles. I lived with them before being recruited by the Empire of Japan as a pilot for the war with America. I crashed in the early morning fog while headed to the attack on Dutch Harbor."

"Aw come on, now your story's going sideways," said Tom. "If that's the case, you're 50 years late to the battle. What kind of game are you trying to play? Whatever it is, we're not amused."

"Silence! You are prisoners of the Empire of Japan," the pilot interrupted. "You will sit still. No talking. You will be turned over to my countrymen tomorrow when they return to retrieve my plane and me," he said with an air of authority.

Will tried to reason with him, "But, this is 1992, not 1942. The war has been over for 50 years! Do you understand this? I don't know who you are, but we have a passenger plane to catch, and we don't have time for this charade."

"Silence! You are prisoners. I ask the questions. You must answer them. If you cooperate, you will be treated with leniency, unlike other prisoners of war to Japan. I trust you understand and appreciate this and agree to cooperate fully. Otherwise, I must kill you."

With that, the pilot produced a handgun and pointed it at Will and Tom. He continued, "I do not want to shoot you, but I will if I must." As he moved quickly towards them, he said sternly, "Now, put your hands behind your back."

As he proceeded to tie up their hands, Will and Tom looked at each other incredulously. He then asked, "Are you military, and why are you here in these mountains?"

Will, trying again to get through to the man, said, "No, as I told you, we have a plane to catch to return home to Richmond, Virginia. We are simply on a hiking trip. Can you let us go, so we don't miss our plane?"

"Ah yes, Virginia. I was in Richmond once." Without another word, he turned and walked toward the rear of the plane.

"And I was worried about bears," Tom said dryly. "Who knew this last, little hike would border on insanity?"

"Seriously, do you think he could be a mental patient on the loose?"

"Maybe, but, I'll tell you one thing he isn't—he definitely isn't a pilot in the Japanese military during WWII."

Will was quiet for a moment before posing a question he feared would make him sound as crazy as the Japanese man.

"Do you think we could have fallen into a time warp in this deep ravine? I've heard about such a phenomenon occurring at odd times in history. I think it's supposed to have something to do with energy, time, and events colliding with elements relating to physics. I don't know exactly, but this oddity that is happening to us is certainly coinciding with the anniversary of a significant WWII battle that could have occurred right here. Just seems weird."

"Geez," Tom said, letting that one sink in for a minute. "I think we have no choice for now but to humor him until we figure out how to get ourselves out of this mess—whether we're in a time warp or being imprisoned by an escapee from the looney bin."

Soon, the pilot returned, and Will was determined to try one more time to reach the rational mind of their captor.

"May I say something?"

"Yes, you may speak," the man seemed calmer now, hopefully more rational.

"We're not American military, and America is at peace with Japan. The war's over and has been for 50 years. We don't know why you think the current date is 1942 because we know for a fact, it's 1992. And, we're very uncomfortable being tied up at gunpoint for no reason."

The pilot maintained his position, "Yes, I understand that you are angry at all Japanese people because we recently attacked your Pearl Harbor, and we are just about to win another great victory at your Midway Island. After that, we will invade America at California, and when we eventually win this war, Japan will rule the world. You will see." Then he turned and walked back to the plane.

So much for the hope of a rational mind, thought Will.

Tom said what they both now knew, "We'd better figure out some way to get away from this nut before he kills us."

"Yeah, unless we want our one last hike in Alaska to also be our famous last words on earth," Will said under his breath.

||

CHAPTER EIGHT
An Escape Back to Reality

"No more talking!" the pilot exclaimed in frustration. "I have been here all day without any food. Do you have food? I'm hungry."

"Yes," said Will, thinking quickly, "We left some food at our camp, not far from here. If you release us, we'll go get it for you."

The pilot narrowed his eyes and looked at Will before saying with an air of superiority, "*You* go get the food. Your friend will remain here. If you tell anyone about me, or if you are not back within one hour, I will kill him. And then I will find and kill you. Understood?"

Will pleaded for Tom to go with him, but to no avail. Tom was required to remain as a hostage. The man then produced a knife and proceeded to cut Will's hands loose.

"Now you go. Come back as quickly as you can, or you know what will happen."

Will nodded to him and said, "Hold on Tom, I'll be right back."

"Please do," his friend said solemnly, not knowing what else to say.

Will hurriedly found the campsite, and thankfully, the food package was still there. He stuffed some beef jerky, trail mix, dried fruit, and chocolate into his pockets with the hope that feeding their captor just might be an important distraction to give them time to figure out some way to escape. Will knew they would need to think and act quickly before something set the nut off. He arrived back at the plane site well within the hour limit set for him by the pilot. Tom seemed happier to see his friend than Will could ever remember. The pilot grabbed the food and began stuffing it into his mouth as fast as Will could get the packages out of his pockets. He washed it down with copious amounts of Sake that he must have retrieved from the plane.

The pilot was so involved in eating the food that he forgot to secure Will's hands, which remained loose behind his back as though they were tied. Tom realized that Will's hands had not been tied up. They figured it must have been the Saki that caused the man to forget a detail of such importance. Whatever the reason, they realized the error might be the break they needed.

Once the pilot finished eating the food, he drank more sake and settled down on the ground underneath a wing of the plane. He appeared to be exhausted, and the men's plan of escape hedged on the hope that he would fall fast asleep. It wasn't long before that was exactly what happened.

Very quietly and with great caution, Will untied Tom, and they slipped away. When they were sure they were out of hearing range, the men ran like they'd never run before. They truly believed their lives were on the line this time. They understood the nature of the bear that came upon them, but how could anyone understand or predict the mind of someone stuck in the past by 50 years?

Will and Tom were concentrating so hard on getting away, that they took a wrong turn and lost their direction. Luckily, they ended up in front of the path to town and the airport. Feeling confident that they had made it back to safety, Will began spouting about what he would never do again when Tom jolted to a sudden stop.

"Did you hear that?"

Then, without warning, there he was. He stood right in front of them, blocking their way to the airport and their safe return. The gun in his hand was pointed directly at them, and they froze in fear as he quickly placed his finger on the trigger.

"I warned you. Now you die."

Never having been in such a deadly position before, the men had no time to do anything more than flinch as the man pulled the trigger. The gun sounded with a loud 'click.' As fast as lightning, he operated the slide mechanism of the gun, chambering a new bullet, and again, he pulled the trigger. With the second misfire, he dropped the gun and fled back down the trail headed away from town.

For a moment, Will and Tom were too stunned to move, but that feeling didn't last.

"Let's go!" Tom shouted to Will.

As they ran towards the path that had been blocked by the pilot, Will reached down and picked up the gun. He planned to give it to the authorities, so the nutcase couldn't come back for it.

"C'mon, man," Tom yelled back to his friend who lagged behind. Let's get down this trail before he comes back."

They didn't stop running until they were within the safety of the airport. Looking at each other in utter disbelief, they couldn't believe what had just happened to them.

"Let's find Sue," Will said. "We need to report this fool to the authorities before he really does kill someone."

Stopping to gather their composure, Tom and Will entered the airport waiting room and were thankful that Sue was the first person they saw.

"Hey, guys, what's… going on—you two look like you've just seen a ghost or something. Here, sit down, and let me get you some water." As soon as they settled down, Sue wanted to hear what happened, "You're both as white as a sheet. It must be serious."

Tom couldn't hold back, "Well, considering we were almost killed a few minutes ago, I'd say 'serious' is the right word for it. We need to report this to the police right away."

"Almost killed? Tom, Will—what's this all about?"

"Tom's right, Sue—some crazy nut tried to shoot us, but lucky for us his gun wouldn't fire, and we got away."

"Hold on. Was this person you call a nut dressed in a Japanese military uniform?"

"YES!" Both men exclaimed at the same time.

"How did you know?" asked Will.

Sue hesitated a moment, and a smile began to cross her face, "I don't want you to take this wrong. I am deeply sorry that you were frightened by Ol' Joe. It's just that most of us locals are familiar with this man's antics. He gets a kick out of scaring hikers, but he's harmless. You don't need to involve the police; they already know about him. I don't mean to make light of your situation, but he's just not a serious problem or a real threat, I should say."

"Well, that's just preposterous, Sue," Will said. "You obviously have no idea what this man is like and what he just put Tom and me through for the last couple hours. This is very serious. Even if he had no intentions of killing us, he could have caused us to fall off the mountain to our deaths trying to escape from him. Would it be considered serious if we'd died? This is no laughing matter, Sue. We're very upset. Do you actually know this man—have you met him?"

"Of course; I understand. Well, everybody *knows* him, or I should say, knows *about* him. We've heard stories, but very few of us have ever seen him for ourselves. In fact, he is quite well known for his reputation, alone. But in actuality, few people, including the police, have actually talked to him. We're told that he pretends to be a Japanese Air Force pilot named, Nakamoto. They say he lives in an old WWII fighter plane that crashed up in the mountains somewhere during the battle of Dutch Harbor.

We don't know how much of this is true, but rest assured you're not the only ones to report contact with him."

Tom wasn't having any of what Sue was saying.

"So, you just allow a local man to hide out in the mountains and terrorize people without even investigating him, and that's okay with the Alaskan authorities? That man almost scared us to death. He also tied us up, held us captive, and when we were lucky enough to escape, he hunted us down and attempted to shoot us. That cannot be okay."

"Sue, I'm sorry, but Tom is right. This man is dangerous, and we insist on filing a police report. Maybe it'll prevent this from happening to someone else with fatal consequences. Since you are a police officer, we'd like you to escort us to the police station."

"Okay, okay, maybe you guys are right. This whole thing about Ol' Joe should be taken more seriously and stopped before someone gets hurt. I agree. I'll be more than happy to assist you in filing a formal complaint."

"Thank you for listening and understanding," Will added.

Tom suggested to Will that they grab a sandwich before going to the police station.

"Okay, you guys get some lunch, and I'll be waiting for you at the station."

"I'm too nervous to eat," Tom said, as soon as Sue left. "I just wanted her to leave, so we could talk about something."

"I'm not hungry, either. What's up?"

"Do you think we should go through with reporting this incident to the police? We might end up having to stay here to testify in court or something. Who knows?"

"Tom, we just made a strong case based on our convictions, and I think we should follow through on this and take our chances. Our actions could save someone's life. You know, as well as I do, that someone like that guy needs to be put away, scaring people like he did us."

"Okay, just thought I'd run that by you. Let's go on to the station then."

Sue was waiting for Tom and Will. They hardly recognized her all decked out in her uniform. She looked different with a pistol and handcuffs on her belt. Will, being of genteel Southern roots, thought such a petite woman looked strange holstering such a big gun. It took the men a few minutes to get used to the new Sue.

She introduced them to Officer J. D. Leheo, a Native American Indian, who had already been filled in on the situation by Sue. He was ready to hear their story.

"Would it be okay for me to tape the conversation for the record?"

"Yes, that would be a good idea, since Will and I won't be here after today."

"You two men aren't the first hikers to make a detailed report about a run-in with Ol' Joe, but few investigations have ever been carried out before, mainly because no harm was done."

Sue overheard them talking about past reports on Joe and walked over to them, "I think a more serious investigation is warranted this time because of the circumstances. People can't be tying people up and threatening their lives. Sounds like our version of harmless Ol' Joe just went off the rails."

After recording Will and Tom, Officer Leheo suggested the four of them go up the trail to examine the plane, "Who knows, we might just run into this Joe character."

Will and Tom looked at each other, and Will took the lead in responding, "As much as we want to help, this has been a really long, tough day for the two of us. Right now, we just want to catch our plane and get home to our wives in Richmond. Our flight is scheduled to take off before too long. I think we've given you enough information to go on to locate the warplane. We'll definitely look forward to hearing what you find out about it and what Joe's game is all about."

As the friends quickly started out of the station, Sue promised she would be in touch as soon as they knew anything.

"Safe flight home, guys."

Finally, Will and Tom were able to head back to the little airport waiting room that they often wished they'd never left, while they were out in the Alaskan wilderness.

"I'm glad we have a little time before boarding to decompress from this hellacious day," said Tom.

"Yeah, I wonder what Grandfather would think about this trip to walk in his footsteps?"

"Well hell, it was almost like *being* in World War II, if you ask me. Think about it. We were told we were arrested as POW's to the *Empire of Japan*—the very thing your grandfather would have given his life to prevent—and, we were damn-near killed by a brutal member of the pretend Japanese Air Force. Not to mention, we witnessed a Zero Fighter Jet for the first time in our lives. I'd say we revisited the war more closely than either of us ever expected, and it doesn't matter that it wasn't real—we didn't know *what* it was, so we went through the emotions of fearing for our lives, just like the airmen you suggested we pretend to be before we left Richmond."

"You know, Tom, you're right! I think we just got a bird's-eye view of WWII and made a little history of our own. Thanks for bringing that to my attention, my friend. I feel oddly better about everything already. I believe Grandfather would've been proud of both of us."

‖

CHAPTER NINE
Detectives in Flight

Will was abruptly awakened from a very sound sleep in the terminal waiting room by someone he thought was trying to shake his guts out—*Ol' Joe!*

Tom was laughing so hard that he could hardly speak a word.

"Will! It's time to board the plane! Wake up!"

"What are you laughing at?"

"You! C'mon, we gotta go—our flight's boarding," Tom barely got the words out, still laughing at his friend. Will, still groggy from having slept so soundly, stumbled along toward the loading gate.

"What's so funny?"

"You were talking in your sleep and swinging your arms all over. I have never seen you so animated. It was hilarious! Please remember that dream, so you can tell me about it when we get seated."

As soon as the men stored their gear and settled into the peaceful refuge of their seats for the long flight home, Tom was itching to hear about Will's dream.

"Okay, what were you dreaming when I woke you?"

"Actually, it was a very frightening dream, thank you. I was reliving the moment when that Japanese fruitcake tried to shoot us. After his gun failed to go off, he drew a second gun in my dream and was just about to pull the trigger when you woke me up. Man, did that ever feel real. I thought I was a goner. I'm glad that's over, and I hope I never have to relive it again—even in my sleep."

The dream brought the ordeal back to Will's mind, and he began to analyze it.

"Do you think there's any possibility we experienced a time warp back there? There were so many things that coincided with our intention to 'walk back in time.' Strange how we came across that WWII plane in the mountains, and how about that fool being Japanese? What are the odds? He sure stuck to his story's timeframe. What do you know about time warps?"

"Not much, man. Seems like a far-fetched idea to me. I've read a little about the subject. Einstein said time doesn't occur in a straight line like we think it does. I guess he basically proposed that time is an illusion. I believe he said it depends on the mass and speed of a particular object—but a World War II fighter plane hurling through space from another time period? I don't know what to think about that.

"The big theory in quantum physics is that an object doesn't really even exist unless somebody's looking at it. It all has to do with atoms, molecules, and particles—hell, I'm an accountant, not a physics expert; that stuff's over my head. But, I bet you our experience is far easier explained without the need to understand physics.

"Think about it. There are things in this picture that just don't add up—like how Mildred discouraged us from hiking very far into the mountains from the beginning. I think there's way more to this story than meets the eye."

"You might be right," said Will. "Hey! Remember how Sue said the Japanese pilot calls himself Nakamoto? Do you remember hearing that name before? Gosh, I can't believe it didn't register before now! Nakamoto is the name JoJo gave as *her* last name...and remember how she told us that *her mom* said it was a *secret?*"

"Yeah, no wonder Mildred was trying to steer us away from

the mountains…or away from that pilot who just happens to have the same last name as her child. Maybe Nakamoto is her attachment to Alaska, and there are more secrets she's hiding."

"You could be right on the money, Tom. Didn't you find it extremely unlikely that he'd forget to tie me back up after I gave him the food? *And*, that he would *take a nap* and risk leaving his prisoners unattended? Our feet weren't even tied up."

"I think you've got something there, Sherlock. I bet you anything he *wanted* us to escape and get the hell outta there. How much you want to bet that gun wasn't even real? He just wanted to scare us away, so we'd never come back! I'm glad you had that dream to open up all these wormholes in the World War II act that character is pulling over on people."

"I can't wait to hear the whole story and see what it's really all about. Let's hold off on divulging our theories until Sue calls us with an update. We'll see what they come up with first. Who knew we'd come all the way to Alaska to help solve a mystery? Ann should've been here. She'd love to put her *Dateline* hat on."

"Well, we said we wanted adventure in our lives," Tom said. "I'd say we got what we asked for, even though it wasn't exactly what we had in mind. I guess we'll find out what story they get when they catch up with Ol' Joe, the imposter, and see what he has to say for himself. The police shouldn't have any trouble locating him."

Will couldn't help but wonder. "Let's hope so," he said. "But Ol' Joe seems to have a plane full of tricks up there in those mountains and local people helping him with them."

The rest of the long flight back to Richmond was happily uneventful for Will and Tom. They couldn't wait to get back to their everyday life. It was easy to miss the old routine when returning from the insanity they just left in Alaska.

The first thing Will noticed as he approached the front door of his home was that there were lights still on. He quietly entered and softly dropping his bags to the floor, he headed toward the sound of the television in the living room. There was Ann; fast asleep. She awoke to the sound of his voice and jumped up to leap into her husband's open arms.

"Welcome home, hon! I missed you so much. Did you have a good time? You didn't stay very long. How was Alaska?"

If only she knew, Will thought to himself.

"It was an interesting time, but we missed Richmond, so we cut the trip short, and am I ever glad to be home? I hope you missed me."

"You know I did," she smiled. It's so good to have you back safe and sound," she said, hugging her husband.

"I can hardly wait to tell you about our adventures. You'll probably have a hard time believing some of them. I think most of it can wait until we wake up—technically, it's already tomorrow, you know. But there's something I have to tell you right now, and then I'll fill you in later on the rest. Tom and I thought we were going to be killed by a crazy man who lived in the mountains. But we now believe he was faking it and not a real threat to our lives. He…"

"What? Oh my God!" interrupted Ann, who was visibly shaken by the word, *killed*. "Did you say you were almost *killed*? What on earth happened?"

"I'm sorry. I shouldn't have said it like that. It turned out to be nothing. I'll tell you all about it after we get some sleep."

"Oh, no you don't, William Sellers! I'm wide awake, so you just tell me what happened right now. I need to know."

Then, as if the news was still sinking into her conscious realization, Ann screeched in an alarmed voice, *"Oh my God! My husband tells me he was almost killed*, and then he wants me to *go to sleep* and wait until later before he tells me about it! Like there's any way I'd be able to sleep after that. Will, do you not realize what a shock this is to me?"

"Okay, I'm sorry," Will said, putting his arms around his wife. "I think I was just looking for a little loving sympathy from my wife, but now that I opened the can of worms, let's sit down a minute, and I will give you the short version."

"Thank you."

"We ran into this Japanese man up in the mountains yesterday morning. He acted like a real nutcase who believed it was 1942. The townspeople call him Ol' Joe, but his name is really Kohei Nakamoto. He proceeded to arrest us as POWs to Japan—if you can believe that—and threatened us with what turned out to be an old, rusty gun that wouldn't even fire. It was all an act, but at the time, we didn't know it. So, it really scared the hell out of Tom and me. Anyway, we reported him to the police, and they're going to let us know when they find him and figure out what he's up to."

"That is just bizarre!" Ann said, dumbfounded by the mere thought of what Will told her.

"Yes, it really is, but as you can see, I am here—safe and sound."

"It sounds like a movie…a crazy movie!"

"Tom and I have our belief about things, but that part of the story will just have to wait until tomorrow—actually, later *today,* because I am tired, and I missed my wife. Now, do we have any brandy in the house? Because if I recall correctly, someone owes me the special surprise I was promised the last time when *that someone* left me holding the brandy."

Giggling at his flirty request and shaking her head at the astonishing tale she'd just heard, Ann looked lovingly into the eyes of the husband she cherished more than ever at this very moment.

"Ah yes, Mr. Sellers, about that. Let me see what I can come up with in the way of redemption. I think you deserve it after all you've been through, and *this* time, *I'll* go fetch the brandy. I'll meet you upstairs—just make sure *you* don't fall asleep."

"Don't worry," replied the cherished husband, "I'm tired, but I'm not *dead tired*," he said smiling.

||

CHAPTER TEN
Murder and the Gun

Tom woke up to a feeling of anxiety and was on the phone early to Will the morning after their return from Alaska.

"You miss me already…"

"Will, you know what we forgot to do….we forgot to tell the police in Dutch Harbor about you picking up that gun. I bet they'd like to know where it is. You still have it, don't you?"

"We didn't forget to tell them. We told Sue, but they didn't ask us for it, and I didn't think to give it to them. I left it in my bag at the airport, by accident, when we went to meet Sue at the station. Hold on a second; I'll go check."

Will searched through his still-packed bags and ran back with the news.

"Yeah, I still have it. Wonder how it got through airport security? Anyway, I plan to call Sue later today, and I'll tell her. She'll know what we should do.

"Okay, sounds like a plan. I hope it won't be a problem. It should have been turned in for evidence, but I didn't think of it, either. By the way, I got the film developed at the Fast Photo Center, and there are some great shots of Sue, Mildred, JoJo, and the bakery. Anyway, I got you copies, and I'll bring them by later. Oh hey, you'll appreciate that the shot you took of Sue hugging me got quite a rise out of Michele. I'm sure you'll make it even worse for me later. Alright, let me know what you hear from Sue."

Will had just picked up the phone to call Sue when the front doorbell rang. He didn't hear Ann going for it, so he put the phone down and headed for the door.

"I didn't do it," Will joked as he opened the door to policemen on his doorstep. The officers didn't crack a smile at his attempt to ease through his nervousness.

"Mr. Sellers, William Sellers?

"Yes, that's me. What can I do for you gentlemen?"

"I'm Officer James Ellison, State Police of Alaska, Anchorage Division. This is Officer Edward Price of the Dutch Harbor Police Department, who I believe you've already spoken with, and this is Officer James Wilson of the Richmond Police Force. We are here as members of the investigation team concerning the recent incident in Dutch Harbor, which you reported to the Alaskan authorities."

Will was so nervous, it took him a minute to respond.

"Wow. Officers, please excuse my shock; I can't imagine what brings you all this way one day after my friend, Tom, and I had to insist on making a report about our troubling experience."

"May we come in? I'll gladly explain why we are here," said Officer Ellison.

"Of course, come in, and pardon my lack of manners. Let's go to the living room where we can sit and talk comfortably."

As they were making their way into the house, Ann called from the kitchen, "Who was that at the door, hon?

"The police."

"No way, you're kidding... Ann's voice cut off, as she entered the living room and saw the officers. As though she'd just seen a ghostly apparition, she stopped and looked at the officers, "What's going on? Why are you here?" she asked with quite an elevated air of concern at the mere sight of them.

Officer Ellison immediately spoke to her, "Please permit me to introduce myself and my fellow officers, Mrs. Sellers, and then we'll get right to the heart of the matter at hand. It is a serious concern, but no reason for alarm."

"I'm sorry, sir, but whenever there are policemen in my living room, I'm both alarmed and concerned."

After the introductions, Will could no longer contain himself, "This is about the encounter we had with that Mr. Nakamoto, isn't it?"

"Yes, but your encounter with Mr. Nakamoto is just part of why we're here. The entire episode has escalated into a much more serious affair, and we need to ask you some questions."

"You said your concern is serious, how so?"

"To put it briefly, someone lost their life during the time you and your friend were in Dutch Harbor, and we're collecting information from everyone who was in the area during that time."

Both Ann and Will gasped in shock. "Do you suspect me of being a party to this death? Is that why you're here?"

"No sir, we're just doing our job and conducting an investigation to see if anything turns up that would be helpful. One thing that does concern us is the gun you reported Mr. Nakamoto as having. We don't have that weapon in evidence, and we'd like to know if you know where it is?"

"Well, yes, I do. Quite by accident, I left it in my bag at the airport before going to make the report, and when no one asked for it, I simply forgot about it. Somehow, it wasn't flagged by airport security, which I still don't understand."

"I trust you have it then?"

"Yes, I still have that old, rusty gun. I had forgotten about it until Tom reminded me of it this morning. It's just as it was when I picked it up from the ground, dirty and rusty."

"Okay, we'll need to test it for firing. But first, let's get to the main interest of the situation involving you, Mr. Sellers."

"Yes, let's do that, please, because I'm starting to feel like I'm the criminal here, and if I were a criminal, I certainly wouldn't have insisted on filing a report about an experience with that crazy Nakamoto clown who threatened my life."

"We understand, and we don't mean to make you feel like a criminal. It's standard procedure when there's been a murder...."

"*Murder?*" Both Will and Ann exclaimed at the same time. Ann threw her hand over her mouth and muttered, "Oh my God," under her breath.

"Yes, and with the gun used to threaten you still in your possession, I'm sure you can understand why we're here." It's our job to investigate a serious crime."

"Of course, we can see the importance of this visit now."

"A Mr. Atkins was found dead in the mountains in back of Dutch Harbor on or about June 3, the same time you and your friend were backpacking there. He was killed with a 9mm handgun, which we believe might be the same kind of gun that was used to threaten you."

"We have also uncovered some additional information about the relationship between Mr. Nakamoto and Mildred Johnson of the Southern Bakery. It appears that they have not only been romantically involved in the past, but they are currently linked as business partners in an illegal operation. You and Mr. Lyman were also friendly with Ms. Johnson and her daughter, JoJo, isn't that correct?"

"Friendly, yes, but that's it. We just met them three days ago for the first time. In fact, it was Officer Sue who suggested we go to the bakery and meet Mildred and JoJo when we first arrived. You have this all wrong if you think it was anything more than that."

"Remember, we're just gathering the facts. Since Ms. Johnson and her daughter are suspected of criminal involvement with Mr. Nakamoto, your relationship with them casts a shadow of suspicion on the two of you that must be eliminated."

"Suspicion of what"

"Of involvement in an illegal drug operation."

"Drugs? That's absurd!"

The Richmond Officer spoke up for the first time, "Mr. Sellers, I'm sorry this is so upsetting to you, but we have to ask, did you have any involvement in or knowledge of the drug-dealing operation going on in Dutch Harbor?"

"Absolutely not!" Will was red in the face now from the suggestion of such a possibility.

"Officer Adams informed us that you picked up the gun Mr. Nakamoto threatened you with. We can't help but wonder how you could have forgotten to turn it over to the police, which in our view would have been the obvious thing to do? Evidence tampering is a chargeable offense all its own, not to mention, the gun now has your fingerprints all over it. If it turns out to be the murder weapon in the Atkins case, it makes you an even stronger person of interest."

"This just seems to be getting worse by the minute. Do I need to call my attorney?"

Officer Price of Dutch Harbor spoke up, "Mr. Sellers, you do what you feel you must do, but remember, there is no evidence of your involvement at this stage. We are simply going through the preliminary motions of figuring out where the puzzle pieces are and how they fit together. But, turning over the gun will help your situation. Do you have it here?"

"Yes, I told you I forgot about turning in that old gun. I don't even know if it's real. I wish you guys had mentioned it when we gave our report."

Will turned to Ann and asked her to go up to their bedroom closet and get the gun from his grandfather's box. She stood and looked hesitantly at her husband for a moment. Ann was rightly concerned that turning over evidence with his prints all over it in a murder investigation might not be a good idea for Will without an attorney present. But she said nothing and disappeared up the stairs.

"While your wife is gone, let me say that this gun is crucial in the investigation. We'll take it back to Anchorage and have it checked out to see if it'll fire and whether it's the actual murder weapon. If it fails in either case, Mr. Sellers, you will no longer be a person of interest in the murder, but, as for the drug operation, that's an ongoing, separate investigation."

When Ann returned, she had a few things she wanted said in defense of her husband. She started off with obvious nervousness fueled by fear.

"Officers, you've got to understand that Will Sellers would never hurt anyone. And, the very suggestion of him being involved with illegal drugs is mind-blowing. He's the administrator of a *children's* hospital. His life's work is helping children be healthy, not getting them or anyone else addicted to drugs. And, if I may add, I hope you can tell from our home and our neighborhood that we don't need to be involved in criminal activities for money. Will is a good provider," she added indignantly.

"I understand, ma'am," said Officer Ellison. "We'll certainly keep that in mind during the investigation, and again, no charges have been filed against your husband."

Officer Price from Dutch Harbor had something else to add, "Mr. Sellers, for your information, Mildred and JoJo are being held for using the bakery as a front for a drug operation. They face multiple charges of drug trafficking. As you know, they are both widely known and well liked. JoJo, who was thought to be 13, is actually 17, and her role in getting young people involved with drugs is especially sad."

"Gosh, that's just terrible. Tom and I really came to like Mildred and JoJo in our short time of knowing them. I can see how the townspeople are shocked over this turn of events."

Officer Ellison continued the questioning, "Mr. Sellers, did you ever meet Mr. Atkins?"

"No, I've never heard his name until today."

Ann wanted to know when they could expect to hear something back from them about clearing Will's name.

"We'll be in touch, but I can't say exactly when," was Officer Ellison's reply.

A soon as the officers left, Ann said, "Oh, Will, do you think there's anything for us to worry about?"

"Ann, you and I know that I would never even think about doing something as wrong as what they're insinuating. So, no, I don't think anything will come of it, but it will be hard not to worry, won't it?"

"Yes, it will. You should call Tom and Michele to let them know what's going on. I'm surprised Tom wasn't contacted. I guess it's because you had the gun."

Will picked up the phone to call his friend.

"Hey Tom, could you come by for a little while, so I can fill you in on the new developments from Dutch Harbor?"

"Oh, did you talk to Sue?"

"No, I wish it'd been that simple. I'll explain when you get here."

"Okay, I'll be right there."

Within 10 minutes, Tom was there to hear what had just transpired, and he was as shocked as Will and Ann.

"Man what a fiasco. I certainly didn't know we'd end up in the middle of a mess like this. Michele will flip out. It just goes to prove that things aren't always as they seem."

"I hope Sue can tell us more about how the plane was involved when I talk to her. Nobody even mentioned it today. I was too wigged out with everything else to even ask."

"What a trip. What a weird, weird trip." Tom said

"Well, you said it'd be a memorable one, and that's proving to be quite true."

Tom went home to bring Michele up-to-speed with the investigation, while Will and Ann tried to recover from what felt like hours of questioning by the police officers. It was something they had no experience coping with, and they were physically, mentally, and emotionally drained. But, Will still wanted to call Sue to see if she had anything to add about the whole situation.

||

CHAPTER ELEVEN
Called Back to Alaska

As soon as Officer Sue Adams heard Will's distressed voice on the line, she began apologizing to him.

"Will, I'm so sorry. I couldn't call you before they arrived to question you. It's against police protocol. I hope you're okay."

"I'm okay, but I'm not sure about my wife. This has been extremely upsetting to her. We gave them the gun, which I brought home by mistake. What can you tell me about this drug operation and the man believed to have been murdered?"

"I can't tell you anything about the man that was found dead, but we located the plane where you and Tom said it would be. We were surprised, like you were, about what good shape it was in. It looks like Kohei Nakamoto has been taking care of it to use for his drug operation and to scare people away from it.

"I don't know if I should be telling you this, but he installed two doors on the plane's underbelly that connected to an inside area of the plane. It was stuffed full of illegal drugs and cash. Nakamoto hasn't been arrested, but he'll soon be arraigned for drug trafficking, and you guys will most likely be called as material witnesses."

"Well, that confirms that Nakamoto wasn't trying to kill us but scare us—and anyone else that came near his stash. It also explains why Mildred was so discouraging of us backpacking up there. We didn't know it was about drugs, but it all adds up now. We're real sorry to hear that she and JoJo are involved. That's sad for the whole community; they're so well-liked."

"Yeah, we don't know the whole story yet, but they're definitely in deep trouble for the time being."

"That reminds me, Sue, did you know that JoJo's last name is Nakamoto?"

"No, I did not."

"She said it was a secret, and we promised not to tell anyone, but I guess all secrets are fair game now."

"Yes, any and all information must come out. I'll let the investigators know that."

Will thanked Sue for the additional information about the plane and the heads-up about possibly having to testify. That was definitely not something he or Tom wanted to hear. They had no desire or plan for a trip back to Alaska.

But plan or no plan, a week did not go by before a special delivery letter showed up at Will's home. Ann called him at the office to let him know.

"Go ahead and open it, hon. Read it to me."

"Okay." Ann took a big breath, hoping for good news. "Here goes:

'Dear Mr. Sellers, the gun you recently provided our officers proved not to be the murder weapon in the death of Mr. Atkins. As of this time, we have not located a murder weapon, nor do we have any reason to believe that either you or Tom Lyman is involved in his murder in any way. We also have no evidence with which to charge Mr. Nakamoto at this time, and therefore, the murder investigation cannot be sustained as part of this case. However, the investigation into the drug-trafficking charge against Mr. Nakamoto will move forward, and your participation in that matter will be required. You and Mr. Lyman are ordered to appear before the Grand Jury Thursday, June 11, 1992, 11a.m. in Dutch Harbor, Alaska to testify to activities pertaining to charges against Kohei Nakamoto on. Thank you for your cooperation, Major William Grayson, Dutch Harbor Police Department.' Well, that was a mixed bag, wasn't it?"

"To put it mildly—Tom's going to be as disappointed as I am to have to go back to Alaska so soon. This is starting to feel like the adventure from Hell."

Tom and Will could not believe they were standing in line to board a plane headed back to Alaska for the second time in two weeks. Neither of them was happy about it. They felt their testimony had already been provided and should have been sufficient for the investigation.

Tom couldn't help but ask, "Now do you wish we had skipped filing that police report when I asked you?"

"If I'd had a crystal ball, I might not have given it a second thought, but who knew this would be necessary? Maybe it wouldn't have been, except for that stupid gun that won't even fire. But here we are, so what can I say, except, I'm sorry?"

"No need for that. I was just thinking how very *memorable* this trip is becoming."

While Tom and Will were mid-air, they had no idea what was unfolding in Alaska. While Will's letter was being delivered in Richmond, Dutch Harbor police had been on their way to the Southern Bakery to arrest Kohei Nakamoto and Mildred Johnson on drug trafficking. But when police arrived, Mildred Johnson informed the officers that Nakamoto had fled the scene, and she didn't know where he was or where he was going.

"Well, that presents a problem, Ms. Johnson, Officer Price said to Mildred. The men from Richmond, Virginia, are on their way back for the hearing, as we speak, and the court is expecting both Mr. Nakamoto and you to be present, as well."

"I understand, and I did my best to reason with Kohei, but I couldn't convince him to stay."

"Did he give you any indication as to where he may be headed?

"No, he didn't."

"We will put a warrant out for his arrest and initiate a manhunt. If you receive any information from him, I would suggest you call the precinct immediately. I think this man has gotten you and your daughter in enough hot water already, wouldn't you agree?"

"Yes. If I hear from him, I'll contact you immediately."

As soon as the plane landed, Tom and Will entered the airport and were greeted by the familiar face of their friend, Officer Sue Adams. But, Sue wasn't smiling like she was when they met her for the first time, less than two weeks ago. There was a distinct look of concern on her face.

"You guys might be in for a little longer stay than expected," Sue said as soon as she got close to the two men. "You're not going to believe what happened. Kohei Nakamoto has disappeared. There's a warrant out for his arrest."

"Holy Toledo, this is insane!" Tom exclaimed.

Will looked like he'd just been run over by a freight train.

"Shouldn't we have expected him to be in custody *before* we got on a plane to Alaska?" As perplexed as he was annoyed by this news, Will continued, "I guess we are just meant to spend a little more time getting to know Alaska. Maybe we can find a good memory to make somewhere."

"Well, we've already made reservations for you at a very nice bed and breakfast called, 'Little Bear.' It's not too far from here. I'll give you a lift," Sue said.

"There we go again with the '*b*' word," Tom whispered under his breath to Will. "Another memory I could have done without."

This time, Will just smiled at Tom, "Yep...the experience we won't *ever be able* to forget as long as you're breathing."

Little Bear was a quaint Inn with well-appointed rooms, fireplaces, and lovely views of the mountains. Much of the artwork in the rooms and throughout other areas featured a small black bear. Upon inquiry of the name's origin, the owners were all too happy to fill them in.

A small black bear began to show up regularly on the grounds when they first opened the establishment. He would come to raid the garbage cans. Unfortunately, people began feeding the little bear, and he became more like the pet of the B&B. Of course, he was still a wild animal, and eventually, he grew too large to be trusted around guests and their children.

To avoid potential problems, the owners had the bear captured and released into the wild, where he belonged. But they decided he had been such an integral part of their early success that they opted to change the name of the B&B from 'The Little Inn' to 'Little Bear' in his honor.

It was a nice story that Will appreciated far more than Tom. But even Tom could appreciate the nice rooms and generously-sized pancake breakfasts, which ranked head and shoulders above their camping experience.

"Yes, this is definitely a step-up from the last night we spent here in a tent."

"You're right about that, Mr. Outdoorsman. Oh, say, before we forget, I guess we'd better let the wives know we'll be staying longer than we expected."

"Good idea. They might appreciate that."

Tom was able to get Michele on the phone, but Will left a voicemail for Ann after several failed attempts to reach her, which worried him.

"Oh, she's fine. Michele saw her earlier in the day, and she promises to look after her while we're gone. She said she'd check on her later and make sure she got your message."

With that, Will let his concerns go. He knew the women were good friends and would pal around together while they weren't there. But Will, Tom, and even Michele had no clue about the dire situation brewing at the Sellers' home.

‖

CHAPTER TWELVE
A Stranger at the Door

It was sometime around mid-afternoon that the doorbell rang at the Sellers' home. Ann was engrossed in a new murder mystery that she hoped to make headway on while Will was in Alaska. Setting the book aside, she headed for the door. She thought maybe it was Michele, but that wasn't a good possibility. Michele never came to the front door. Ann hoped it wasn't someone selling something.

Peeking through the small peephole, she saw a well-dressed man standing on the front porch. Not recognizing him, she asked without opening the door, "Yes, can I help you?"

The man replied, "Hello, ma'am, my name is Sideki. I'm here to speak to your husband."

Ann knew to be careful with strangers, "What's this about?"

"I wish to apologize to him in person for something I did. If he's not here, I can come back at another time. Could you open the door and speak to me for just a minute?"

Checking that the safety chain was in place, she cracked the door ever so slightly, "My husband isn't here at the moment. What's this business about an apology?"

"It's about some trouble I caused him in Alaska."

"Alaska? You met Will in Alaska?"

"Yes, ma'am."

"Wait, I know who you are. *Trouble?* You're that pilot that tried to *shoot him*—but his name wasn't Sideki, it was, umm...."

"Nakamoto... Kohei Nakamoto."

83

"YES! That's the name. You, Mr. Nakamoto, tried to kill my husband. What nerve you have showing up at our home. In fact, you're wanted by the police in Alaska at this very moment for drug trafficking. I'm going to call them right now!"

"Please don't do that. I can explain everything if you give me the chance."

"Why in the world would I give you a chance, much less trust anything you said?"

"I didn't murder anyone, ma'am, nor did I deal drugs. The attempt to kill your husband and his friend was just a ploy to scare them away from the mountains. I think you'd understand if you'd just hear me out."

"How did you find out where we live?"

"I'm friends with some of the locals in Dutch Harbor, and I've been to Richmond before. I got your address from JoJo Johnson. She had gotten it from Sue Adams because she wanted to write your husband a thank you note for his kindness in promising to help her visit Virginia one day."

The mention of Sue and JoJo in relation to a kindness by Will made Ann feel a little better. Her curious mind was wondering why this man was really in Richmond at their home. She was very interested in what she could learn from talking to him. *I'd love to hear his version of the story,* she thought. *He doesn't appear to be dangerous, but looks can be deceiving. Maybe, I could get some new details about the drug operation to help the case, so Will and Tom can come home faster.*

"My husband is due back any minute, so you don't have much time. You wouldn't want him to find you here, trust me. I don't make it a habit of talking to strangers, especially under these circumstances, but we have security cameras throughout the inside and outside of our home. Plus, my neighbor has a very watchful eye."

"I know my word means nothing to you, but I have no reason to harm you. I just want to tell my side of the story and apologize to your husband. I'll be gone after that."

"Come in," Ann said opening the door. "I'm interested enough in your story to give you a few minutes of my time."

"Thank you."

Ann led the man to their living room to sit down.

"I appreciate that you let me come in to talk to you. My real name is Kohei Sideki. My parents live in Kobe, Japan. My sister and her husband are naturalized American citizens, who live in Los Angeles. I lived with them when I attended UCLA."

Ann could believe that, as she took notice of the man's polished conversation and ability to speak almost-perfect English, which she attributed to his attendance at a prestigious American University.

"For some time now, I have been on my long journey home to Japan while visiting many places in America, including Dutch Harbor, Alaska. I have a keen interest in WWII because my uncle served our country in the Battle of Dutch Harbor in 1942. While I was there, I got a job as a guard working for Mildred Johnson, who owns The Southern Bakery on Main Street."

"Yes, I know of Mildred and her daughter, JoJo."

"My job was not to guard the bakery, but an old warplane in the mountains. I was told the abandoned plane was used by the bakery to store goods, and it was my job to prevent any looting. I had no idea that drugs were being stored there. I invented the idea of acting like a WWII pilot, who thought it was 1942, so people would think I was crazy and leave the area right away.

"Many of the people I scared away told their stories to the locals, who gave me the name Ol' Joe. It all seemed harmless until your husband and his friend involved the police because of the old gun I pretended to try and shoot them with. I found it under the plane, and I used it as a prop in my act. It wouldn't shoot anyone. I want to assure you that I was not involved with

85

the drugs. I was simply hired to guard the contents of the plane and nothing more."

Ann could have been impressed by the man's charm, but she reminded herself that many people are gifted in this way, especially con artists and criminals. She knew it wasn't wise to be taken in by his words alone. Often the truth lay beneath the spoken word. What she was most interested in was his motivation in trying to convince her of his innocence. She pretended to believe what he was telling her to see if the truth would surface.

"I'm relieved to hear you say that you had no intention to kill my husband. I wouldn't want to think I was sitting here in my own home with a murderer and a drug lord."

"I know you have no good reason to believe me, but I'm pleased to hear you may give me the benefit of the doubt."

Ann found herself intrigued with the man. And, though she wasn't about to believe everything he said, she also knew it was possible that some of it could be true. *What if they were wrong about this man's role in the drug trafficking? Could Mildred have been the real mastermind?* These were the thoughts rolling through Ann's mind.

She also kept reminding herself of the pending charges against him in Alaska and how he had frightened Will and Tom, putting their lives in potential danger.

"Well, I have taken far too much of your time. Perhaps, I could come back tomorrow when your husband is home. That will give you time to digest what I have told you, and hopefully, your husband can forgive me for the distress I caused him and his friend by pretending to be someone I wasn't."

Ann's curiosity had been piqued. She thought progress had been made in having him think she believed him. She hoped more valuable information would come out if the conversation was allowed to continue. So, she agreed to a second visit the following day at 5 p.m. when she led him to believe that Will would be home. Surely, she reasoned, if he returned with the expectation that her husband would be there, it was an indication that he was sincere about apologizing to him.

Kohei Nakamoto left with the promise to return, knowing full well that Ann's husband and his friend, whose lives he had threatened, were actually in Alaska waiting on him to be located and returned for his hearing on drug trafficking.

But, he had a plan, and so far, the plan appeared to be working.

||

CHAPTER THIRTEEN
Charmed by Sweet Wine

Ann thought a lot about what Kohei Nakamoto had told her. If only Will was home to hear his story, but at the same time, she knew he would not be able to be objective. At times, she admitted to herself that the man's spiel sounded rehearsed, like a speech he'd prepared. Yet, a part of her found his story somewhat compelling.

She knew she couldn't tell anyone about this situation. Even Michele wouldn't understand why she'd allow a wanted criminal in her home and trust him to be alone with her. But, she didn't feel threatened by his presence, and he'd already left on his own once, without being asked to leave.

Ann considered handing him over to the police, but the sleuth in her kept wondering what might come out of this opportunity. Just maybe, she'd be able to get to the real truth of the matter faster than the police. She'd be careful.

One more evening to talk about things with him could help her decide the best course of action to take. That sounded reasonable to her—and playing detective gave her something of an adrenalin rush, she had to admit.

The next day seemed to go by very slowly to Ann. But, 5:00 finally arrived, and Kohei promptly showed up as promised. Ann was surprised and a little suspicious of his intentions when she saw that he came in with a bottle of wine.

"I hope you don't mind that I brought along a bottle of French wine. It's of very high quality and one of my favorites."

Ann also noticed that Nakamoto wore more casual clothes for this visit, and he seemed more relaxed, overall. His change in demeanor reminded Ann briefly of the analogy of letting a fox in the hen house. She sized up his look. The gray slacks and blue blazer he wore spoke of class, and he certainly didn't act like a typical criminal. But, Ann's guard was up.

"I'm not sure wine is appropriate for this meeting, but thank you, nevertheless."

"Should we wait for your husband before opening it?"

"Will is otherwise engaged, after all. We can just go ahead, and I guess a little wine couldn't hurt anything."

Ann watched carefully as Kohei opened the new bottle of wine and poured it in the two glasses she had given him.

As they sat facing one another in the living room, sipping the wine, their conversation slowly digressed to a somewhat more personal nature. Time flew by unnoticed. The small talk about their lives didn't feel as uncomfortable to Ann, as she would later think it should have. Part of her mind considered whether she was falling under the spell of a charlatan. *Stay on guard*, her intuitive thoughts reminded her.

"Have you had time to think any more about what I've told you and whether or not you can believe me?"

Between sips of the wine, which she had to admit was extremely delicious, Ann said, "I certainly sympathize with your side of the story, but I can't help but wonder why it's important that I believe you?"

Before Kohei could answer that question, Ann heard the clock chime in the hall and realized the time. She stood immediately and said, "Oh my, I'm sorry, but I have plans with a friend for dinner."

"If you'll allow me to come by for a short visit tomorrow, I'll answer that question for you, Ann. Will 5 p.m. work again?"

"Yes, that will work."

As soon as Kohei left, Michele came in through the back door to the kitchen. She and Ann had planned a girl's night out with dinner at a favorite neighborhood restaurant to catch up on things, since the guys were out of town. Michele didn't waste any time getting to the question burning a hole in her mind.

"Ann, I couldn't help but notice a strange man at your front door the last two afternoons. Who was that?"

"Oh, let's get settled at the restaurant, and I'll fill you in on all sorts of things." Ann was actually feeling a little woozy, which surprised her because she hadn't drunk much of Kohei's wine.

Thankfully, the restaurant was nearby, and since they had reservations, they were seated right away. After the women ordered their meals, with Ann passing on the wine, Michele was ready to hear what was going on.

"I thought maybe he was the Japanese man you guys had as a visitor last year, so I didn't bother calling. Was I right?"

"Well no, not exactly," Ann said with a chagrinned look on her face. "He says he is Kohei Sideki…but our husbands would recognize him as Kohei Nakamoto from Dutch Harbor."

Michele stopped drinking her wine and stared at Ann with a look of pure horror and disbelief on her face.

"*What*! You mean the man who tried to kill Will and Tom?"

"Yes, that's the man. He claims to….."

"Ann, have you lost your mind? That man is wanted for possible murder and drug trafficking, and you just let him into your house? This is insane—I'm calling the police right now."

"No, Michele. Don't call them yet. He's been telling me his version of the story, and he's been rather convincing. I'm trying to figure out what his motivation is. I think he is trying to win me over and use my influence with Will in some way to help him. I just don't have it figured out yet."

"Ann, I know you love mysteries, but this isn't a *Dateline* episode. I think there is something wrong with this picture, and you could be in grave danger. I know that your judgment is normally very sound, so I'm going to give you the benefit of the doubt and not call the police right this minute. But, you need to fill me in and give me your sincere promise that you'll keep in touch with me about what's going on. I'm sorry, but I'm finding this all very hard to wrap my head around. What in the world would the guys say?"

"I know, I know. I understand how you feel. You have my promise to keep you informed. But don't be too far from your phone, in case I need you in a hurry, okay? And, thank you, Michele, for being there for me."

"You're welcome, of course. I know you'd do the same for me. I just can't understand why you're doing anything like this, and I'm worried about your safety."

"One thing did seem odd, and you're the only person I can tell this to. Before you came over, we were drinking some really fabulous wine that Kohei brought with him. Before I knew it, we were talking casually about our personal lives, like we were friends or something. And, for some reason, it felt totally natural to me at the time. Though looking back on it now, I know it wasn't normal at all. What do you think that's about?"

"Okay, now you're scaring me. Did you drink too much wine?"

"I don't think so."

"Was it a new bottle?"

"Yes, I watched him remove the seal."

"Look, I don't know this man, and I'm certainly not in a position to judge him. But, I know what our husbands think about him, and I know both of them pretty well. Just remember, many lifetime criminals are master manipulators. There has to be some hidden agenda, or he wouldn't be hanging around you like he's been doing. Just think about it, Ann. Put your investigative hat on—and you most definitely shouldn't be drinking wine with him."

"Okay. You're right, as usual. I'll think about it. And, next time I meet with him, I'll be far more careful."

||

CHAPTER FOURTEEN
A Heart-to-Heart

Ann felt in her bones that it was time for a reckoning between her and Kohei. Deep inside somewhere, she knew that she was being used for something, and it was high time for all motives to be put on the table.

Kohei was right on time, and once again he came with that special wine, in hand. Ann grew evermore suspicious that the wine was intended to loosen her up for something, but she didn't want to alert him to her suspicions by not drinking at all. She would just be careful to consume very little of it, as Michele had warned.

As Kohei and Ann were chatting, Ann suddenly thought it would be a good idea to also eat some food to help lessen the effects of the wine. She asked Kohei if he'd like something to eat to go with his wine, and he agreed.

While they were eating, Ann reminded Kohei that he said he'd explain to her why it was important that she believe his side of the story about his involvement in the Dutch Harbor drug operation.

"Yes, thank you for reminding me. In Japan, apologizing is a cultural requirement. We find it highly disrespectful and unacceptable not to say you're sorry for intentional wrongdoings or even for accidents that you caused unintentionally. I know it will be hard for your husband to accept my apology for my actions toward him and his friend. Since I haven't been able to meet with him yet, I hope you are able to believe me and that will help convince your husband of my sincerity and my innocence."

"Well, I can't promise that Will or Tom will agree with what I have to say about any of this. I can only say that I will relay what you have said about everything. You still have the courts to face in proving your innocence on the drug-trafficking charge. *They* will certainly not listen to anything I have to say."

As they began to clean up their dishes, they found themselves side-by-side for the first time. Before Ann realized what was happening, she found Kohei's arms around her, holding her close to him. She wriggled around to resist his advances, and within a few moments, they both backed away from each other.

Ann was shocked that some part of her was finding this man's interest in her even the least bit flattering. She felt herself falling briefly into a confusing emotional abyss, before she snapped to her senses and escaped his embrace. Soon afterwards, the reality of what happened disturbed her greatly.

"Kohei, what just happened? It must be the wine because it's not like me, at all, to allow something like that. I love my husband, and this is not acceptable behavior."

"Yes, I understand. I'm sorry. It won't happen again."

"No, it certainly won't. What were you thinking?"

"Honestly, I wasn't thinking," Kohei began. "It was just an emotional response. I have come to like you very much over the last couple of days, Ann. Suddenly, I just felt very close to you. I apologize for my actions. I know that in America, men are not quite as free with their feelings, but in Japan, we are very expressive. Again, I apologize that I made you feel uncomfortable. Please forgive me.

"I must commend you, Ann, for your high moral ethics. That's something I greatly value in a person. Your husband is a lucky man to have such a beautiful and trustworthy woman for a wife. No doubt, you will have beautiful children and a long, happy life together.

"I have plans as well. With my degree in Engineering from UCLA, I have a good job in auto-manufacturing waiting for me in Japan. I'm excited about a new start, and I want very much to put all the drama of Dutch Harbor behind me."

"Kohei, I wish I could help you with that, but I can't imagine how that would ever happen. You know they're looking for you to face the court hearing you skipped out on, correct?"

"Yes, I'm aware of that."

"For the life of me, I still can't understand your reasoning in coming here?"

Kohei looked deep in thought for a few moments, as if he was deciding his next best course of action to take with Ann, especially now that he had, inadvertently, admitted to being deceitful. He decided that coming clean would mean the most to her and serve him best.

"I was afraid. I knew they would be looking for me, as they have no other suspects in that small town except local people who are their friends. I came to the East Coast because I knew they would be concentrating on the West Coast and would never expect me to hide out in your home in Richmond, Virginia. That would be the last place they'd think to look.

"I also knew that your husband and his friend would be called back to the hearing and not be home. JoJo confirmed that for me when she gave me your address."

"Well, you certainly had all the details nailed down, now didn't you?"

"You will do what you have to when your life's on the line, and you know you're not guilty. You mentioned helping me. I do have a proposal for you—one that could help me get back home to Japan to restart my life. I hesitate to ask because you may feel that it compromises your integrity, but I assure you that you won't have anything to worry about, if you agree to help me, that is."

"Hmmm, does that mean I *will* have to worry if I don't agree to help you? Just tell me what it is that you want me to do, Kohei."

"I need you to accompany me to the airport and pretend for us to be a couple until we board the plane together. You won't actually go to Japan and shouldn't be required to say anything. It'll just be for the sake of appearances—to help us look like an ordinary couple on a trip to Japan, so I won't draw any undue attention. They won't be looking for me to be part of a couple. Then, right before the plane is set to depart, you'll ask to get off for a family emergency and simply return to your home. Then, you'll never see me again."

"Well, that's some plan you conjured up. I'll have to give it some clear-headed thought and see what jeopardy my participation might put me in, not just with the authorities, but with Will. How do you think my husband is going to feel knowing that I helped the person escape who has caused him so much trouble and distress? I will give it thought overnight. You may call me for my answer in the morning at 9 o'clock."

"Thank you, Ann. I appreciate that you'll consider helping me get back to my homeland and a fresh start."

And with that, Kohei Nakamoto was gone. Ann, however, was left with an agonizing night to analyze her thoughts over a stressful decision she needed to make quickly.

I could use some of that special wine right about now, Ann thought. Instead, she picked up the phone to call Michele. Two heads would be better than one on this decision.

||

CHAPTER FIFTEEN
The Night before D-Day

The phone rang at the Lyman's home with no answer. *Darn, I really need Michele's input on this tonight,* Ann thought. She went on to spend what seemed like hours considering all the things she and Kohei had just discussed, especially his plan of escape, which was foremost on her mind. Her decision loomed large. She analyzed every aspect of her participation that she could consider on her own, except one—what Will would think about it.

She never made big decisions without his input, but her gut said loud and clear that he would not be onboard with the plan at all—none of it. After all, Kohei scared both Tom and him to death, almost literally. She knew he was stressed about the whole matter, and even knowing about this would increase his stress load by one-thousand-fold, especially if he felt his wife had befriended that very same man. What if he knew that while he was sitting in Alaska waiting for them to find Kohei Nakamoto, the fugitive was hiding out at his own home *with his wife*?

Suddenly the magnitude of the situation was hitting reality for Ann. Thinking more clearly than she had in days, she now felt very disloyal to the man she loved more than anyone in the world. If the shoe were on the other foot, she might have a hard time understanding or believing Will's motives. Would he be able to forgive her for spending time and drinking wine with this man? These were all scary questions to which she had no answers.

Even though, she had initially convinced herself that she was trying to help, sadness now filled Ann's senses. She wondered if that was the whole truth. Now she was just feeling very confused by her actions. She'd put aside all idea of calling Will in Alaska when the phone rang, causing her to jump out of her seat.

"Oh Michele, thank God, it's you!"

"Goodness gracious, what's happened? Are you okay?"

"Yes....no....I don't know. Can I come to your house? I need to talk with you right away. I need your brain."

"Sure. Gee, you're scaring me. Come on over right now."

Michele was waiting for Ann at the kitchen door, "Come on in."

They could barely sit down before Ann started pouring her heart out to Michele.

"You just won't believe what happened tonight. Kohei and I were going to have something to eat with the wine. I thought that was a good idea, so even the small amount of wine I was drinking for the sake of appearances, wouldn't have an effect on me like it may have before. Then all of a sudden, he grabbed me in a tight hug! I got away from him and told him, in no uncertain terms, that kind of behavior was off limits. He apologized, and that was that. But, then he dropped a bombshell, and that's the part I need help with right away."

"Oh my God, Ann—what kind of bombshell?"

Ann filled Michele in on Kohei's escape plan. Michele looked stunned, and she was sure her shock was written all over her face. She couldn't believe what she was hearing from her best friend. Still, she wanted to tread softly into this new territory that Ann was considering because she wanted her friend to hear her.

"I suppose you have your reasons for even thinking about helping this man, and who am I to judge or second-guess you? But if you want me to play devil's advocate, I will."

"Yes, tell me whatever you're thinking."

"Okay, as you probably already know, I'm deeply concerned about the situation you're in right now and how you became wrapped up in such an unusual mess. What I'm about to say is based on what I've heard from you. Remember, I have never met Mr. Nakamoto. But, I believe he devised a scheme to get into your house and into your head with charm, well-spoken English, nice clothes, and wine under the pretense of saying he wanted to apologize to Will. But to tell you the truth, he probably knew all along that Will was back in Alaska for the hearing."

"You're right. He admitted that."

"Then he knew you were alone, and the apology motive was a bunch of hooey, of course. And about that business with the hug tonight—that was just a ploy to see how deeply involved you are with him emotionally.

"By the way, that special wine has been a tool to make you feel comfortable with him from the beginning. I know there have been times you have hoped his story could be true. But, he comes across to me as an extremely conniving, deceitful man with an ulterior motive to escape the charges in Alaska, and he saw you as a sitting duck he could use to make that happen."

"Wow!" said Ann. "I have been going over everything while waiting to hear from you, and I think you just hit a grand slam on the whole scam. I feel like such a gullible fool—like so many of the *Dateline* victims might feel—if they had lived! I wish I'd had your perspective earlier in his game."

"Actually, Ann, you may not have been able to hear or believe me then. I think sometimes we just have to go through things ourselves to really understand them."

"I guess you're right, but this is a painful lesson, and it's not over! What am I going to do? Do you think I should go along with his plan and go to the airport?"

"Do you think you really have a choice? It sounds like he is pretending that you do, but we also know what a good actor he is. Have you thought about what he'll do if you refuse? He's invested quite a bit of time in grooming you to help him escape."

"No, I guess I haven't given it enough thought. I suppose I have been in denial by trusting his nature, but I could be dead wrong—or let's just say, wrong! He did make a comment about 'how people will do anything they need to when their lives are on the line.'"

"If you refuse to help him, and he forces you to go, that would be coercion, which I think would protect you from being held accountable in aiding and abetting the escape of a wanted fugitive."

"Oh my God, I didn't even think about that!"

"You also have to think about how your decision is going to make you feel later about helping him escape and how Will is going to feel about it, too."

"I know, and that worries me. I don't want to disappoint Will. There's so much riding on this decision. Michele, do you think Will is going to be able to forgive me for letting that man into our home?"

"What's done is done. What happens tomorrow is yet to be seen. There's no point in worrying about either one. I do believe things have a way of working themselves out. Will loves you and trusts your judgment. It may take him some time to understand the decisions you made. He doesn't need to know everything. Some of it may be as hard for you to explain, as it would be for him to digest, so I'd skip those parts—like that hug."

"Thank you, Michele. You are such a good and wise friend. God knows where I'd be without your help on this. Please keep this between us, okay?"

"You got it, pinky-swear—just between us! Good luck tomorrow, and let me know what's happening because I will be on pins and needles until I hear from you."

"I will do my best. Good night, Michele. Please say a prayer for me—on second thought—pray without ceasing!"

||

CHAPTER SIXTEEN
True Nature Revealed

Ann woke up early around 7 o'clock a.m. to the sound of birds singing. She hoped that was a good sign. She wanted to be wide awake when Kohei called. After talking with Michele the night before, Ann felt much stronger. She needed to have this conversation with Kohei, so this drama could be over and done with.

She was a little worried about how he might handle her decision, so she was glad she'd be telling him over the phone that she couldn't help him escape. But at precisely 9 a.m., the doorbell rang, and when Ann looked through the peephole, she was surprised to see Kohei standing there.

Without thinking, Ann opened the door as usual, "Didn't we say that you'd call me for my decision?"

"Actually, you said that, but I thought this was something that should be done face-to-face, since we've become friends."
Ann felt uncomfortable with this change-of-events, but she decided to go ahead with what she'd planned to tell Kohei.

"Kohei, I hope that you will be exonerated by the truth of your innocence, if that is truly the case, and I hope it is. However, I cannot be a party to helping you escape from the country before you've had your day in court to prove your innocence.

"My participation in something illegal isn't the right thing for me to do, and I'm afraid that particularly in this case, it would also cause big problems for my marriage."

Kohei no longer looked like the cool, collected class-act he had been over the last few days. He didn't blow up in rage, but Ann could tell by the look on his face that he easily could have.

He turned and looked directly into Ann's eyes and spoke to her in a controlled manner.

"Ann, I was afraid you might say that, and it's very unfortunate. I have done everything I can to have you make the right decision on your own for both of us, and I can't tell you how disappointed I am that you didn't. I have spent a lot of time visiting with you to make you feel comfortable with my request for your help."

He took a deep breath, peered out the window for a moment, before continuing.

"I have been a gentleman in every respect, with the exception of one hug, which I explained to you. And now that you have dishonored our friendship, I have a few things to let you in on.

"The *special* wine was not special because it was French or of a high quality. It was special because of the drug I put in each bottle I brought here."

Ann started to speak, but Kohei put up his forefinger to silence her.

"I'm not finished. You'll have your turn. I could not be certain that you would do as I asked you, so I took measures to ensure it would go the way it must for my safe return to Japan. I have been drugging you with a small amount of relaxation substance in the wine to help you trust me. It's a process often used by men who want to take advantage of women sexually— something by the way—I never did to you."

At first, Ann just stared into space in total disbelief of the nightmare she willingly allowed herself to be a part of. She felt herself becoming angrier by the minute. Then, she suddenly raised her hand, with her palm facing him.

"Let me get this straight. You have been drugging me with the wine that was sealed, and I watched as you opened every brand new bottle, every single time I drank any?"

"Yes, that's correct," he responded with a smirk.

"How?"

"It's quite ingenious, actually. I learned it from my days in the pharmaceutical industry. I used a very small drill bit to make a tiny hole in the bottom of the bottle. Then I inserted a small needle-syringe filled with a common, non-dangerous drug that I injected into the wine. I sealed the hole by pressing wax into it, so the bottle showed no signs of being tampered with."

Ann gasped incredulously, "Well, here I was thinking of you as a charming, well-cultured, and honorable Japanese man who was potentially being wrongly accused. I welcomed you into my home, and that is how you repaid me. Now, I feel like an idiot fooled by a devil. I can't tell you how angry that makes me! It never occurred to me that you had it in you, Kohei Nakamoto, to do something so vile and dishonorable to me, especially after I trusted you, in spite of all of the serious charges against you. I guess your drugged-up *special wine* did the trick."

"Yes it did, but I didn't have to use anything but *my natural charm* to get you to welcome me into your home, now did I? Wonder what Will would think about that?"

That made Ann furious, "Shut up!" No longer did she have any kind feelings for this imposter. She knew he was everything they thought he was.

"So, since you're toting drugged wine around with you to take advantage of women, I presume you are the drug dealer the police say you are?"

"Well, let's just say I was somewhat more involved than I took credit for with you," Kohei smiled, "and actually, the operation is quite larger and more successful than the '*Hokey Harbor*' police force will ever figure out.

"But soon with your help, sweet Ann, that will all be behind me when I get out of this country. And just to let you know, since I haven't been formally charged with a crime, you can't get into any trouble for your part in my escape—not that I really care."

"As if that makes me feel any better about helping you; what happens if I refuse?"

"Oh Ann, that wouldn't be a good idea," Kohei said menacingly. "Then, I will have no choice but to force you to do so. I really hope it doesn't come to that. You haven't been exposed to my ugly side, yet."

Kohei leaned in towards her and pretended to whisper a secret, "I'm not *nearly as charming* as you think I am."

"I can see that now," Ann shot back, as bravely as she could. She felt as though she had been tricked by the snake in the Garden of Eden. She silently admonished herself for being played a fool. *I should have known better. So much for my good judgment,* Ann thought.

"Now, I have already told you my plan to get me back to Japan. So, let me ask once more, have you come around to the right decision in helping me?"

"I will do so only under protest and not of my own free will. I will consider this a forced participation, do you understand?"

"It matters not to me what you call it, dear Ann," Kohei chuckled.

"I have one more question of you, Kohei Nakamoto."

"What's your question?"

"You had every opportunity to take full advantage of me, sexually, yet you didn't. Why?"

"Oh I'm sorry," he said condescendingly. "It sounds like that's bothering you? Once that little hug went awry, and you freaked out, I didn't want to risk it. Sexual pleasure wasn't my motivation for being here, and your reaction showed me that you weren't far enough under the effect of the drug to make it easy or enjoyable.

"That's what tipped me off to come in person today. You failed the drug test. Too bad for you—we could've had a *really* good time."

Unlike Ann in the use of profanity, she muttered out loud, "Damn you! You just get creepier all the time!"

"Call me what you will."

Kohei had more unexpected news for Ann. "I'm glad I did come in person to hear your refusal, which I expected. We have a new plan. We're leaving today. The taxi will be here in 20 minutes to take us to the airport, *my darling.*"

With that Kohei bellowed a hearty, smug laugh.

||

CHAPTER SEVENTEEN
Secret Surveillance

Michele hadn't heard anything from Ann since the night before. But now that she knew what Nakamoto wanted Ann to do, she felt she was in good shape to watch out for her friend. Michele had not told Ann the full truth. She had become concerned about her friend right after Will and Tom left to go back to Alaska. The girls had always kept in close touch when their husbands were out of town, but that hadn't been the case this time. Red flags flew when she started noticing the Japanese man visiting her friend and neighbor's home on a regular basis. So she took matters into her own hands.

Unbeknownst to Ann, Michele set up a secret surveillance program from her upstairs bedroom window, where she kept a watchful eye through her binoculars over the Sellers' home. She had been taking photos of the comings and goings of the stranger, in case anything happened.

After asking Ann about the visitor and detecting the confused emotional state she was in, Michele suspected foul play and felt her surveillance was the right thing to do. But, as soon as she heard it was Nakamoto who had been visiting, she decided to get the police involved before something terrible happened to her friend that she, alone, couldn't prevent.

She only knew the name of one policeman, Officer Price in Dutch Harbor. She picked up the phone and called him with the number he had provided Tom. She explained the general situation to him. After listening carefully, he became obviously alarmed when he heard the name, Nakamoto.

"We are searching for Mr. Nakamoto right now and were unaware of his whereabouts until this moment, thanks to you. Your friend, Ann, may very well be in grave danger, and you may be, too. You did the right thing by calling. Hold on a minute. We are now in the process of contacting the Richmond Police Department to see if they'd be willing to cooperate with us to set up an active surveillance program, perhaps a stakeout.

"Okay, I've just been informed while we were talking that they've agreed to set up a stakeout immediately. Officer Cullison will be in charge of the operation. He will contact you at your home phone and arrange a way for you to communicate with him. Please don't attempt to contact him in person. We don't want to compromise our cover. This contact you've just made with me may have a direct result in justice for Mr. Nakamoto. Please be careful, young lady, and thank you for calling."

Things began to happen fast once Officer Cullison became involved. He called Michele with the news that the Richmond Police were currently on duty with a stakeout, constantly observing Ann's house. He gave her a phone number that she could use to contact them at any time. She was asked to discontinue her private surveillance project for fear that she might accidentally alert Mr. Nakamoto, thus, blowing their cover. She was also reminded to make no attempt to contact the surveillance officers, in person, for obvious reasons.

Michele thanked Officer Cullison for his prompt action, and she gave thought to the request for her to back off her personal surveillance. With such a great view of Ann's house from her bedroom window, Michele decided she should continue watching, but she would exercise great care, so as not to be detected. There was always a possibility that she'd recognize something uncommon to Ann that they might miss.

An early riser, Michele was on duty watching Ann's house when she saw Nakamoto at Ann's door. She remembered Ann telling her that she would give him her decision by phone, so she was surprised to see him there this morning.

A couple hours after Kohei arrived, Michele saw a cab pull up to the front of Ann's home. She picked up her binoculars and got a clear view of Kohei putting luggage on the front porch. She knew immediately what was happening. They were preparing to leave for the airport to execute Nakamoto's escape plan. That could only mean Ann was being forced to participate.

She picked up the phone and dialed the number given to her by Officer Cullison. He answered immediately. Michele began, almost breathlessly, to describe what she had just seen.

"Calm down, young lady." Then in a professional voice, he said, "We've got eyes on them already. Richmond Police are on their way to Richmond International Airport. By the way, Kohei Nakamoto is now definitely being sought on suspicion of murder, as well, because of new developments in the Dutch Harbor case. So, you can see how imperative it was that you called us when you did. Nakamoto is a dangerous character."

Michele watched as Kohei and Ann carried bags to the waiting taxi. The driver placed them in the trunk. As the vehicle eased away from the driveway, Michele saw Ann give a glance back at her home, and they were soon out of sight.

Within 25 minutes, the taxi arrived at the airport terminal building. With the bags dropped off for check-in at the entrance, everything seemed perfectly normal. Quite a few passengers were going about their business, as time for their departures drew near. No one seemed to pay any attention to Kohei Nakamoto and Ann. They appeared to be like any ordinary couple starting a trip, just as intended.

There were a few security guards and police officers strategically placed about the terminal, but nothing seemed out of the ordinary. The couple took a seat. Kohei hoped the tension between the two would go unnoticed. Soon, boarding began for the flight to Japan. They picked up their carry-ons and entered the passageway that led to the plane. They took their seats, which were just a few rows back from the front of the cabin.

As soon as the plane was fully loaded and all passengers were seated, a well-dressed gentleman appeared, accompanied by a police officer. The man was introduced to the passengers as the Lt. Governor of Virginia, which drew applause from most passengers. One man could be overheard saying the man was not the Lt. Governor, but the comment was generally ignored.

The gentleman shook some hands, making his way to Kohei and Ann. As he reached out to shake hands with Kohei, who showed no signs of alarm, the senior flight attendant in front of the cabin door motioned for Ann to come to her. Ann excused herself and walked toward the attendant who immediately took her by the arm and briskly walked her into the passageway where a police officer awaited her.

As soon as Ann was out of sight, the gentleman, with the police officer at his side, showed his badge to Kohei and identified himself as a member of the Richmond Police.

He asked, "Are you, Kohei Nakamoto?"

To which Kohei answered, "No."

"Then what is your name?" asked the officer.

"Kohei Sideki."

"Mr. Sideki, would you please come with me?"

Kohei was caught, and he knew it. *Damn it*, he thought, *How did she manage this?*

The police officer was prepared in case Kohei offered any resistance, but there was none. He arose from his seat where escape had seemed eminent and accompanied both officers off the plane. As they appeared outside, the uniformed officer could not contain himself and practically shouted into his walkie-talkie to the team on surveillance, "We've got him! The suspect is in custody." It was a good day, indeed, for all involved in the uneventful capture of Kohei Nakamoto.

On the plane, the attendant nonchalantly announced to the passengers that the drama, which many passengers didn't even notice, was over. "The plane is now cleared for takeoff. Please be certain your seatbelt is fastened. Enjoy your flight."

Ann was escorted to a waiting police cruiser by two officers, one of which was the stakeout officer, Stan Cullison, who said, "Boy am I glad we caught that bastard! Oh, excuse me, ma'am."

"No need to apologize to me. You should hear what I think of that jerk," replied Ann.

Officer Cullison introduced himself to Ann and said, "It's so nice to meet you in person. I feel like I already know you, although we've never officially met. I know your friend and neighbor, Michele Lyman, who helped set up this sting operation. I've never met *her* face-to-face, either. She and I have been watching after you and your house. She has been keeping tabs on Mr. Nakamoto for several days and called..."

"Did you say you've been working with Michele watching my house?"

"Yes, I have."

Ann said, "Holy smoke! Oh my goodness, thank you so much. You and Michele may very well have saved my life."

"Yes ma'am, that was the plan," he said with a smile that could light up the airport.

A cavalcade of police cars arrived at the Sellers' home to deliver Ann safely from the airport. There were police cars parked everywhere, even in the yard, many with their flashing blue lights still on. The scene had all the looks of a crime scene in progress.

Ann exited the car and was accompanied by two officers to her front porch. When she approached the front door, it burst open in front of her, and Michele stood on the other side, grinning from ear-to-ear. Not a word was spoken as they embraced. It was a long, hard hug.

"Welcome back, girlfriend."

"Oh, Michele, I love you. Thank you. You have no idea."

"Hey, you're welcome. I'm just glad you're safe. You told me to watch out for you, but you should've known I was always on it. We're like family."

The relief in the successful end of a terribly stressful situation showed on both their faces. It was time to celebrate, but all they wanted to do was rest and have quiet.

The officer-in-charge took Ann by the arm and led her into her own living room to a gathering of police officers and a few news reporters from the local affiliates of national news organizations—NBC, ABC, and CBS.

"Here she is folks, safe and sound."

He then motioned for Michele to join them, and he introduced her as the neighbor who initiated surveillance on her own and alerted police. They attributed her swift actions as a concerned citizen to the capture and arrest of Kohei Nakamoto.

"These two brave women are to be commended for their assistance in the apprehension of a dangerous fugitive from justice wanted in Alaska for evading arrest on charges of drug trafficking and murder. He is currently on his way to a nearby correctional facility until he is returned to face those charges in Dutch Harbor, Alaska.

"Without the help of these two citizens, Mr. Nakamoto may very well be on his way home to Japan right now. Let's give them a very much-deserved round of applause."

All of this attention came as a pleasant, but overwhelming, surprise to both Ann and Michele. They were just relieved and overjoyed to have this all behind them, so they could get back to their normal lives.

"If anyone needs further information on the case, please contact the Dutch Harbor Police Department, where it will be permanently filed under the Dutch Harbor Incident," the officer-in-charge announced to reporters.

Will and Tom had been trying to get through to both of their wives to let them know that the hearing had been canceled for now, and they were on their way home from Alaska. It seems they just missed the airport takedown and pulled up, instead, to the aftermath of excitement in their neighborhood.

The Dutch Harbor police did not want to risk the success of the sting operation underway in Richmond, and therefore, neither man knew anything about the arrest of Nakamoto and the part their wives played in it. The operation was the real reason the hearing was called off, and they were put on a plane home.

At the sight of all the many police cars, both men began to panic, their eyes wide in fear. Never in all the years of living in their quiet neighborhood had they seen more than one police car at a time, and it was usually passing through on its way to someplace else.

"Will, what in Hell's name do you think this is about?"

With no place to park, they drove into Will's yard. Will jumped out of the car before it came to a complete stop and began running toward his front porch. He quickly identified himself to the police and went into the house yelling for Ann. Much to his surprise and embarrassment, he burst right into the crowd of reporters and policemen assembled in his living room. In the center of it all were Ann and Michele.

"Will," Ann screamed, at the sight of her husband, "Here, I am!" she waved.

They managed a quick hug before Will asked, "What in the world has happened? Are you and Michele alright?"

Before she could answer, the lead officer announced, "This is Mr. Will Sellers, the husband of Ann, one of our heroines of the day." More applause ensued.

"What are they talking about? I feel like I'm on a movie set, instead of in my home."

Ann said, "Will, just calm down for a few minutes until all these people leave. Then Michele and I will fill you and Tom in on everything over some much-needed pizza and beer."

"Okay, hon," he was just so happy to be with her, after his initial scare of seeing the police cars.

Tom had come in and reached Michele, "Can we get this place cleared out, please? I think it's going to be a long night. I could use a beer about now to settle my nerves before we hear what all this commotion is about."

A reporter overhearing Tom's comments, said to both men, "Didn't you gentlemen hear? Your wives were instrumental in the arrest of Kohei Nakamoto, a dangerous fugitive from Alaska."

To say the looks on the faces of Tom Lyman and Will Sellers were those of absolute shock and utter disbelief would be an understatement.

Yes, it was definitely going to be a long night, a very long night at the Sellers' house. These two couples had mountains of catching up to do.

||

CHAPTER EIGHTEEN
Revelations Old and New

Following a restful weekend, Ann rose early on Monday morning. In many ways, it felt like a normal day with rapidly fading memories of the hectic days beforehand. It was good to be back to her familiar routine of fixing breakfast and getting Will off to work.

She poured herself another cup of coffee and sat down at the kitchen table to read the morning paper. She was looking for the story about capturing Nakamoto at the airport when the phone rang. She knew immediately who it was.

"Good morning, Michele," she said, and with a big happy sigh, "Isn't it great to be back to our regular lives?"

"Oh my goodness, I just can't tell you. Good morning to you, Sunshine," Michele said, beaming through the phone line.

"Say, have you had your breakfast yet? I have one hot cinnamon bun here with your name on it. How about I bring it over, and we can have our Monday morning girlfriend talk as usual?"

"Ann, no cinnamon bun needs to have my name on it! You know I am watching my weight, and I don't mean watching it go up." But, after a short pause, Michele said, "Oh, what the heck, bring that bun on over. I'll start watching my weight tomorrow."

Ann set out right away to the Lyman's, where Michele stood in the open door waiting for her friend and the cinnamon bun. Grabbing one more cup of coffee each, they sat down at the kitchen table and got started. The talk for today would certainly center on rehashing some of the highlights of Ann's last meeting with Kohei Nakamoto that Michele had not yet heard about.

"Did you see the morning paper?" asked Ann. "I haven't had a chance to read it yet."

"Me neither, but we know pretty much what the papers will say," Michele said with a laugh. "Right now I'm more interested in your last visit with Kohei, which I'm sure, I won't find in the newspaper. You know that whole thing didn't seem like you at all, Ann. Do you think you were infatuated with him?"

"No, that wasn't it. I was infatuated by curiosity. My investigative mode went into high gear, and for some reason, my rational mode became disengaged. I mean, I was impressed with him enough to be able to consider his story, and he was nice to me, which made it hard to think of him as such a bad person. I really thought he might not have been guilty, at first. And then later, I became consumed with trying to figure out his motives for coming to our house. Too much *Dateline,* I guess. Turns out, I'm not that great of an investigator. You, on the other hand, Michele, would make an amazing detective!"

"You think? Why? What happened? Was I right—did he slip you a mickey?"

"There you go, right again, Detective Lyman."

"That *special* wine—I knew it! I thought about that when you said you felt funny after drinking it. Did that sleezebag drug you with some kind of date drug that would let him have his way with you?"

"Well, yes, he did drug the wine—I'm not sure what kind of drug it was. He said he only added small amounts. Remember, he was drinking it, too. He did it to make me like him enough to trust and believe him, so I'd be open to his suggestions and allow him to be in control—but it didn't work."

"What do you mean?"

"Well, you helped immensely by telling me not to drink the wine, which I should have known not to do. And, you were right about that hug being a test. He was actually testing to see how much of an effect the drug was having on me. But, because you and I had talked about being careful of drinking the wine, I was not consuming much of the drug either.

"So, thanks to you, the hug didn't turn into something I would have deeply regretted. He called the hug a 'drug test' to see if I would be easy to have a good time with."

"Asshole! That's horrible. I knew you were in danger. I could feel it. Then what happened?"

"After I failed the 'hug-drug test,' he stayed focused on his true motive to use me to help him escape, instead of taking me for a 'free ride' in the bedroom.

"The next day, he showed up at my house instead of calling me because he figured he'd have to force me to help him escape. He didn't feel he could trust me, since I wasn't drugged enough.

"Of course, he was right about that, and he turned into quite the mean and ugly villain when I refused to help him. I got to see him for who he truly was. That man needs to be in jail."

Michele just stared at Ann with her mouth open. "It's seriously a good thing that we went out to dinner the night before and talked about that whole thing. Praise God everything went as well as it did."

"Praise you, too, for being the real Nancy Drew here. Are you sure you don't watch *Dateline*?"

"Obviously, I don't need to!"

"That's for sure, and I will never make a questionable move without consulting you first in the future, Detective Drew! In fact, let's draw up a mental pact right now that we agree on. We'll call it the Ann and Michele Pact, or AMP, for short.

"Every time there's a questionable move the other needs to make, we'll promise to check the other's advice for a yes—AMP

Up or an AMP Down—for no. And we have to consult with the other before going against the advice. What do ya' think?"

"I love it," Michele agreed! "Can you believe all that drama is truly behind us? Our guys don't have to go back to Alaska for any hearing, and it's back to work for them, where there may not be a lot of adventure—but there's no danger either! Kohei is in jail, we're safe and sound, and hey, we turned out to be heroines, to boot!"

"Yeah, sounds like the guys might be ready to give up on backpacking after this. I think Will and I are going to partake in some much-needed celebration time tonight. You and Tom should, too. We've all been through a heck of a lot of Alaska! By the way, do you have a bottle of brandy you could spare?"

"Why, yes ma'am, I do."

In Celebration and Reflection

More than a month has passed since Will Sellers and Tom Lyman returned for the last time from their WWII adventure in Dutch Harbor, Alaska. At first glance, their backpacking journey did not seem to provide them with the satisfactory experience they had hoped to have. But upon closer inspection, they could see that it had given them all they had hoped for, and quite more.

Never would the men have believed they could've gotten such an authentic taste of World War II in the present. In fact, having had time to reflect upon their journey, they recognized some surprising correlations to the past that they could not see while going through it, which is often the case for so many life experiences.

"Well, one thing is for sure, Will, we will never look back on our trip to Alaska, and say it came up short on excitement, now will we?"

"No, you called it when you said it was going to be the 'adventure of a lifetime.' Luckily, we lived to tell about it. But,

Tom, I've had some really interesting thoughts about the irony of what happened to us there."

"Like what? What do you mean?"

"Well, think about it. The original battle of Dutch Harbor was an attack on Americans by the Japanese in a major world war."

"Okay."

"So, here we go off to Dutch Harbor to walk in my grandfather's footsteps, *at the very time* he served on that battlefield, 50 years ago. The meaningful time we are there adds to the mystery of how we end up encountering a dangerous, ego-centric *Japanese* man, in an authentic *WWII flight suit,* employing the same kind of *Zero Fighter plane* used in *1942* to run a *modern-day attack on Dutch Harbor.* Just like his ancestors, he's hoping to cash in on his perception of the wealth and abundance in America."

"Yeah, yeah—except his weapon of choice is drugs, instead of bombs," said Tom.

"Bingo! It almost seems like the sense of a time warp that I kept feeling was more of a parallel reality, to an extent."

"Except—there's no war going on right now."

"But Tom, there is." We're in healthcare. We know as well, if not better than most, that there is a very real ongoing war against drugs in America, and we're not winning. We just got a glimpse of that war wrapped up in WWII dressing!"

"Wow! That's an amazing analogy I would never have thought of. No wonder you're in charge at the hospital."

"You know what really astounds me? What an incredible coincidence that Grandfather's death, along with its proximity to the special WWII anniversary, occurred precisely when we were seeking adventure in our lives and caused us to change our trip plans. All three events came together with perfect timing to provide the catalyst that sent us to Dutch Harbor, where we were able to help win a battle in the war on drugs."

"That is so perceptive, Will. What do you think made you see how all those things fit together?"

"Heck if I know. Maybe it's Grandfather talking to me. The whole realization just dawned on me from out-of-the-blue. Grandfather and I always had a very special connection. He even said in one of the letters to me that '*not even death would break our bond.*' He always seemed so proud of the man I grew up to be, and I do believe he's proud of the journey we just took," Will said, with tears in his eyes.

"Well, I think it goes without question that we may have really helped the people of Dutch Harbor by revealing the covert drug operation, especially when other people—even the police— were willing to just let the Ol' Joe character slide," Tom said.

Epilogue: New Adventures on the Way

Tom and Will may not have realized that by answering the call to adventure, they encountered similar challenges with lessons learned, as have many heroes who embarked upon a journey of self-discovery. Their wives learned a few lessons, too.

Some viewpoints the couples found meaningful to their lives going forward were:

- ❖ No matter how far you travel to find excitement, there's no place better to return to than home and the treasures you find in your own backyard.
- ❖ Everything is not always as it seems, but if you take time to reflect upon the illusion, often you may see a reason—even a blessing—for its appearance in your life.
- ❖ Overcoming the greatest of personal challenges can render transformative experiences, from which one may emerge a stronger individual.

With lessons learned and the adventure completed, the two men sold all their backpacking gear and discovered plenty of excitement waiting for them at home. There were some joyous new experiences to come, even in an old Southern town where nothing ever seems to change. In fact, some were already on the way.

Friday evening, Will came home from work at his regular time, and Ann was waiting in the kitchen for him. There stood his beautiful wife with the biggest and brightest smile he'd ever seen on her face. He knew instinctively that something was up.

"Honey, how would you like to hear the pitter-patter of little feet running around the house?" She giggled, awaiting his response, still grinning, wide-eyed.

"Please, not a dog, I...wait a minute, *oh my God*, Ann—you're pregnant, aren't you?"

Without waiting for an answer, Will grabbed Ann and swung her around and around in pure, joyful ecstasy, as happy as two people who wanted to be parents, so badly, could possibly be.

"Oh hon, I am so excited and happy. I love you so much. I need to be more careful with you in your condition, though."

"Not yet, that'll come later," Ann said. "We should call your grandmother. She'll be so happy. You should be the one to tell her, and I'll take care of calling Michele and Tom."

"Okay, I'll call Grandmother! By the way, I will be doing all the grocery shopping, cleaning, and other strenuous stuff. You'll need all the rest you can get."

"Don't be silly. I feel fine. We can just lead our normal lives for a good while yet. I'll need to rest later, so don't wear yourself out too early."

"Say, wonder if it's a boy or girl?"

"There you go again, being silly. It's too early to tell."

"But it's not too early to start thinking of names, is it? If it's a boy, I kinda' like William, Jr. We could call him Billy like Grandfather called me."

"Great—and if it's a girl?"

"I know what we *should* call her."

"What?"

"Brandy... with an *i*—How's that? I think Brandi would be cute, don't you? But, for the next nine months, my darling, no more brandy for you!"

After dinner, they went to separate rooms to make their calls. Will gave his grandmother the joyful news, while Ann called Michele and Tom.

"Michele, guess who's having a baa--by?" There was an unexpected pause on the other end of the line.

"Did Tom tell Will? I wanted to be the one to tell you..."

"Michele! Are *you* pregnant?"

"Isn't that what you're talking...Ann, *are you having a baby, too!*

Nine months later, right on time, Brandi Sue was born to Ann and Will...two weeks after that, Thomas Jr. came on his own time to Tom and Michele.

With the best kind of new adventures already begun, ones that would last a lifetime, the two couples and best of friends began embarking upon the journey of parenthood in Richmond, Virginia.

The adventures of World War II in Dutch Harbor, Alaska, past and present—though never to be forgotten by any of them—were but a distant memory in their rearview mirrors.

....

"Say, Will, maybe we'll do some camping with the kids in the backyard one day. What do ya' think?"

Will just shook his head, "I think that sounds like a good plan, buddy."

ABOUT THE AUTHORS

William Selvey is a World War II Veteran who served as a member of the Army Air force (AAF), stationed in Germany from 1945-1946. He holds a Bachelor of Science in Biology from Concord University, a Master of Science in Biology from West Virginia University, and a Master of Science in Hospital Administration from the Medical College of Virginia/Virginia Commonwealth University School of Medicine.

He is recognized as a founding member of the Children's Hospital of The King's Daughters in Norfolk, Virginia, where he was the hospital's first administrator in 1961. Today, it is known as the leading children's hospital in southeastern Virginia and the only free-standing children's hospital in the state.

After retiring, he and Bertie Sue Selvey, his wife of 42 years, co-owned and operated The Kensington Bed and Breakfast for 29 years. They hosted many authors visiting the Richmond area and a few celebrities in town to shoot movies.

At 91 years young, Bill writes songs that he performs with his baritone ukulele. *Parallel Reality* is his first book as an author. He lives in Richmond, Virginia.

Deb Childs has a BA in Business Management from Mary Baldwin University. She began her writing and publishing career in 1999 as an award-winning magazine publisher, highlighting stories of business excellence in the Richmond region.

Her first book won a Global E-book award for her story of love and loss and gained attention in Europe. Deb enjoys her work as a ghostwriter helping others get their stories well-told and published. Her books, *Last Promise—Losing My Heart~Finding My Soul* and *A Spirit in the Doorway,* can be found through booksellers on Amazon.com and at **debwchilds.com**